C

M

N

QY

C

O

SPECIAL MESSAGE TO READERS

THE ULVERSCROFT FOUNDATION
(registered UK charity number 264873)

was established in 1972 to provide funds for research, diagnosis and treatment of eye diseases. Examples of major projects funded by the Ulverscroft Foundation are:-

- The Children's Eye Unit at Moorfields Eye Hospital, London
- The Ulverscroft Children's Eye Unit at Great Ormond Street Hospital for Sick Children
- Funding research into eye diseases and treatment at the Department of Ophthalmology, University of Leicester
- The Ulverscroft Vision Research Group, Institute of Child Health
- Twin operating theatres at the Western Ophthalmic Hospital, London
- The Chair of Ophthalmology at the Royal Australian College of Ophthalmologists

You can help further the work of the Foundation by making a donation or leaving a legacy. Every contribution is gratefully received. If you would like to help support the Foundation or require further information, please contact:

THE ULVERSCROFT FOUNDATION
The Green, Bradgate Road, Anstey
Leicester LE7 7FU, England
Tel: (0116) 236 4325

website: www.foundation.ulverscroft.com

BROKEN PROMISES

The greatest day of Carolyn's life has arrived: she is to marry her beloved Henry. But when she gets to the church, it becomes clear that something is terribly wrong. The groom has disappeared! Devastated, Carolyn is supported by her brother and his girlfriend as she tries to pick up the pieces of her life. When she meets kind, caring Jed, she feels as if she really is over Henry — but is this just a rebound? And will she ever find out why she was jilted at the altar?

CHRISSIE LOVEDAY

BROKEN PROMISES

Complete and Unabridged

LINFORD
Leicester

First published in Great Britain in 2014

First Linford Edition
published 2016

A catalogue record for this book is available
from the British Library.

ISBN 978–1–4448–2946–4

Published by
F. A. Thorpe (Publishing)
Anstey, Leicestershire

Set by Words & Graphics Ltd.
Anstey, Leicestershire
Printed and bound in Great Britain by
T. J. International Ltd., Padstow, Cornwall

This book is printed on acid-free paper

1

Carolyn sat in the taxi with her brother on their way to her wedding. She could hardly speak for the excitement of it all. This was the happiest day of her life: the day she had been awaiting forever, it seemed.

'Nearly there, love,' said Paul. 'Half an hour or so and you'll be Mrs Henry Jefferson.'

Carolyn smiled and took his hand. 'Thanks for being here for me. Mum and Dad would have loved to see this day, wouldn't they?'

'I'm proud to be here. And yes, Mum and Dad would have been as proud as I am. Even prouder, if that's possible.'

Carolyn was wearing her wedding dress, a simple strapless gown that showed off her figure perfectly. It was short, and she was wearing a tiny veil. Her long hair was done up on top with little curls falling down either side of her face.

'Here we go,' she said. 'Wish me luck.' Paul grinned at his sister and held her hand.

The taxi drew up outside the church and a photographer appeared as if by magic. 'Smile, please. I'd like a shot of you getting out. That's right. Help her, will you — Paul, isn't it?' He nodded. 'That's right. Straighten your veil.'

'Is Henry here?' Carolyn asked.

'I'm not sure,' replied the photographer. 'I'm detailed to get pictures of you.'

'I'm sure he will be.' Paul sounded quite certain, and Carolyn smiled at him. He helped her out of the car and took her arm, ready to walk her down the aisle. In the porch, there was something of a holdup. Her chief bridesmaid looked concerned.

'Nothing to worry about, but Henry seems to have gone missing,' she told Carolyn. 'Only for a moment, I'm sure. He was here before but seems to have disappeared for now. Shall I go and check?' she asked Paul.

'I'll go,' he said. 'Might look better. Stay there a mo. I won't be long.'

Carolyn felt her heart start to thump uncomfortably. There must be something major wrong, or why else would Henry have gone? She began to shiver, her light wedding dress seeming inadequate in the circumstances. She tossed back her veil, handed her bouquet to her bridesmaid, and opened the door, marching down the aisle in a rather business-like manner. The congregation started murmuring to each other and one or two of them rose from their seats, trying to intercept her. She brushed them aside, stopping at the altar.

'Where is he? Where's Henry?' She looked around her. And where was the best man?

One of the groomsmen came over. 'I think he may have gone to the loo or something,' he murmured.

'With his best man? How long ago?'

'Well, I'm not sure. He went out about five minutes ago. Jerry followed him.'

'Could you please go and see what the problem is?'

'I think Paul went out after them.' The groomsman clearly didn't quite know what to say.

'I know he did. Dammit, *I'll* go out after them, then!' She marched through the vestry, where the vicar was standing, visibly worried and looking helplessly at the rear door.

'What's going on?' Carolyn demanded.

'I'm not sure. Your groom, Henry, disappeared through that door. His best man followed him, and then your brother.' She glared at the poor man and charged out of the door herself, just in time to see Henry disappearing along the road into a taxi.

'Henry?' she called in a pitifully broken voice. 'Paul? What's going on?'

'It seems Henry has absconded,' said Paul, running over to her. 'I didn't hear exactly what he said, but he's just gone.'

'So the wedding's off?' she asked.

'I'm sorry, but it looks like it.'

'But why? Did he give a reason?'

'He simply said, 'It's no good. I can't do this to her.' I'm so sorry. What do you want to do?'

'After I've caught him and killed him, you mean?' Carolyn said, glaring at Paul and struggling to hold her tears at bay. 'Oh, I don't know. I really can't believe it. I mean, why? What have I done to deserve this?' She was by now shaking vigorously with a mixture of shock, cold, and anger.

'Here, borrow my coat,' Paul said. He hung it round her shoulders and she nodded her thanks. 'I suppose we'd better go back inside and tell everyone.'

'What about all the food?' she asked. 'At the reception?'

'I don't know. Shall I tell them to go and eat it?'

'Why not? It's all been paid for. I think the booze was on sale or return, so maybe they can pay for that.'

Paul stared at his sister. Since when had she become so practical? 'Okay, I'll go and tell them. What about you?'

'I can't face everyone out there. I'm going to go back to the flat. See if I can find Henry and ask him what he's playing at. Here, you'd better have your jacket back. I'll sneak out through here.'

'Why don't you wait for me? I'll tell everyone to go to the reception and then I'll come back with you.'

'No. You go with them. I need someone to sort it all out. I'll be fine.' She rushed out of the rear door of the church and headed toward the waiting bridal car. The driver was somewhat bemused, but did as she told him. He dropped her back at the flat he'd collected her from less than an hour ago.

'Thanks,' she said. 'Take the rest of the day off.' She leapt out and ran up the stairs to the flat she'd shared with Henry for the past several years.

'Henry? Henry?' she called. 'Are you here?'

Carolyn looked round the flat she'd left with such high hopes that morning. Her clothes lay on the bed where she'd left them. Sadly, she stripped off her wedding dress and changed back into her everyday things. She looked in the wardrobe and saw that everything that was Henry's had gone. He must have come straight here from the church and removed all his clothes.

'You bastard,' she muttered. Then she sat down and began to cry, and carried on crying for almost the rest of the afternoon. She thought of the reception and all their friends eating their carefully selected menu. She hoped the band would have gone home. What a disaster. Damn Henry. He could pay for the lot. She could see no reason why she should lose out. How could anyone do this to someone he claimed to love? She began to cry again and lay down on the bed, sobbing till she finally fell into an exhausted sleep.

★   ★   ★

She woke up to the sound of knocking and sat up, thinking she'd ignore it. She didn't want to speak to anyone — except Henry, who she'd like to tear several strips off.

Someone was calling her name. 'Carolyn? Carolyn! Please answer me. Come on. You're doing yourself no good at all.'

It was Paul. Slowly, she rose from the bed and went to open the door.

'Thank you,' he said. 'At last. You look a wreck.'

'Thanks a lot. What do you want?'

'To make sure my little sister is all right.'

'I'm fine. Just dandy. Ready to swing from the lamp-posts. Hunky dory. Now, off you go.'

'No way. I'm staying here till I'm certain you're all right. Now, what is there to eat?'

She thought for a minute. 'There's nothing in. The fridge is turned off. Remember, we were going away on honeymoon. I emptied the lot and cleared everything out.'

'No tins or anything like that?'

'There may be some soup. But I don't want anything. Did people go to the reception?'

'A few of them,' Paul informed her. 'Nobody was very enthusiastic, except Uncle Sydney. He was ready to eat for Britain. Even took a load of stuff away with him. The caterers were pretty decent. They're not charging for some of the stuff; said they'd take it back and freeze it, and save you some money.'

'That's up to Henry. He's paying.'

'Assuming he's ever brave enough to show his face again.' Paul contemplated his sister. She did seem quieter now. Less angry; calmer. 'Carolyn . . . look, I don't think you should stay here. Why don't you come home with me? Stay for as long as you like. It'll mean you won't be on your own; and when Henry comes back to earth, he'll know where you are. Leave a note here and let him come back when he's ready.'

'Oh come on, Paul. Be sensible.

Henry's gone. He's out of my life. I don't even pretend to understand why, but his things have all been removed from the wardrobe, and . . . ' Tears filled her eyes and she began to sob again.

'Come on. Pack a few things and let's go.'

'I've already packed. Where's my suitcase?' She remembered packing her bag for the honeymoon. Henry had it in his car. Where was that? 'Henry had it in his boot. Do you know where his car is?'

'Maybe it's down in the car park? I doubt it, actually. He'd have needed it to take his stuff away. Has he left your luggage somewhere?'

'I don't know. Maybe it's in the bedroom.'

'Haven't you looked?'

'No. Never even thought about it.'

'Well, go and look. You can pick it up and bring it with you.'

'If it's there, I'll have to unpack and put in some sensible stuff. We were going to the Seychelles. I've got bikinis and . . . and . . . Oh, never mind.'

She went into their bedroom, and there, sitting on the other side of the bed, was her suitcase. Henry must have brought it back when he collected his things. She opened it and fresh tears immediately pricked her eyes. Her flimsy nightie for the wedding night at the top, and all her new things for an exotic honeymoon beneath it, were more than she could bear to see. She snapped it shut and looked for an overnight bag. Finding one, she stuffed in some jeans and a couple of tops, clean pants, and toiletries from the bathroom. That would do.

'Good girl,' said Paul. 'Come on. I'll stop and buy some food on our way. Mel will be away for a few more days, so it'll just be the two of us. She was gutted to miss your big day, though it seems she hasn't missed anything.' Mel, his long-term girlfriend, was a flight attendant.

'I wonder if he'll have cancelled the

honeymoon?' Carolyn mused angrily. 'Damn him. Why on earth has he done this? We were supposed to be staying at a hotel near the airport. Should I phone them, do you think?'

'I'll give them a call.' Paul asked for the number and dialled it on his mobile. 'Hello? I'm calling on behalf of Henry Jefferson. Sorry? Oh, I see. He's already called? Okay. Thanks.' He switched off the call. 'Seems he's beaten you to it. I bet he's also called the airport and the honeymoon hotel.'

'If not, he can pay for the lot,' Carolyn snapped. 'Come on then, let's go.' She couldn't bear to be in this place any longer. Too many memories. She hadn't expected to see it again until after the honeymoon with her beloved Henry. Tears were streaming down her face, but she didn't care.

Paul locked the door and gave her the key. She followed her brother out to his car, then dumped her bag onto the rear seat and got in.

'Come on, love,' Paul said quietly.

'Wipe your eyes and blow your nose.'

'You sound like our parents,' she said, almost laughing. 'Time I gave up crying, so you're quite right. Henry can go to hell, for all I care.'

'Good girl. What do you fancy for supper? I'll go and buy something now.' He drew into the car park of the supermarket and stopped near the door.

'Anything you like,' she muttered. She sat staring round, wondering why she was there. They should have been enjoying everyone's company at their reception. Then they were going to drive to Heathrow and their hotel for the night. *I will not cry again*, she told herself, gritting her teeth.

Moments later, Paul arrived clutching a carrier bag with various food items in it. He also had a large box of tissues, which he gave to her. 'Just in case,' he said with a grin.

He drove the short distance to his place and they went inside. He lived in a delightful cottage at the edge of the town, with two bedrooms and a cosy lounge.

'Thanks, Paul. It's good of you to put up with me.'

'No worries, sis. Now, you make yourself at home while I go and sort out supper. I've got a couple of steaks and some salad stuff.'

'Sounds lovely,' she told him, though the thought of eating anything revolted her.

She went upstairs and into the spare room. The bed was made up and ready for her. She took out her jeans and tops and put them away into the drawers, then slumped down onto the bed and glanced at her watch. It was almost eight o'clock.

'Oh Henry, where are you? Why have you done this to me? To us?' she muttered. She swallowed hard, determined not to start crying again. When she went into the bathroom and saw her face in the mirror, she realised she looked awful. Her eyes were red and swollen; and the mascara, so carefully applied that morning, had run in rivulets down her cheeks.

She picked up a flannel and began to scrub at her face. The wedding makeup gradually came off, and she looked much better. The flannel was decidedly mucky now. She unpinned her hair and shook her head, allowing it to fall down into its normal style. Then she went downstairs and apologised to Paul.

'Sorry, but I've ruined your flannel. I'll buy you another one.'

'Don't be silly. It'll wash. I've poured you a glass of red. Drink it while the steaks are cooking.'

'Thanks, Paul. I'm sorry I'm such a wet weekend. I promise I'll soon be better.'

'I'm sure you will.'

2

Henry had been on the run for the past twenty-four hours. He had collected his things from their flat and tossed them all into the back of his car. He hated doing this to her. Carolyn did not deserve it, but if he had stayed and gone through with the wedding, he dreaded what might have happened to her. What had those men said? That he needed to keep his side of the bargain or they'd take it out on Carolyn. He was so ashamed of himself and what he'd been drawn into. He'd been so stupid.

It had all begun some weeks ago. Henry had been for a drink with several colleagues after work one evening. They'd all gone home, and Henry was about to head off too. He finished his drink and made to stand up when a man he hadn't seen before came and sat beside him, pouring him another glass of wine.

'Henry, isn't it?'

'Do I know you?' Henry had asked.

'Not yet, you don't. I'm hoping to put that right very soon. You work for Phoenix, don't you?'

'Yes. What's it to you?'

'I have a proposition to put to you. Make us both a lot of money. And I mean a lot. More than you could ever dream of. You're getting married soon. I know all about you. About Carolyn too.'

'I don't know how you've found all this out. But forget it, I'm not interested,' said Henry, slightly disturbed that this stranger knew so much about him.

'Don't rush away. Surely you'd like a few hundred thousand to add to your bank account? Buy a nice place to live for the lovely Carolyn. Nobody loses out, I promise you. Only Phoenix, and they can well afford it. I just need some information from you. Just a few amendments to your company's pro-file.'

'I'm sorry. You've picked the wrong man. Now, if you'll excuse me.' Henry tried to rise but the man stopped him.

'You really don't mean that, Henry. I know that if you really think about it, you'll be willing to help. There will be consequences for both of you if you don't.'

'You sound threatening. I don't like that.'

'Threatening? Not at all. I'm just offering you the opportunity to make a lot of money. I'm talking about a few alterations here and there, that's all.'

'What do you mean, alterations?'

'Good. You're getting interested. I like that. You're a smart man. That's why I chose you. It's all quite simple . . . ' He launched into a description of Henry's job and what he would need to do. As the man had said, it would be simple enough, and Henry would be paid a lot of money. It would mean they could buy a really nice flat, or even a house.

'You do make it sound quite easy,' admitted Henry. 'And how would I get the money?'

'I'll organise payment directly into your account.'

'And you're sure nobody could trace it back to me?'

'Not if you're careful. How about it?'

Henry asked for time to think about it and the boss agreed. He suggested meeting the following evening, and they parted.

Looking back, Henry knew he should never have agreed to even consider the proposal. It really hadn't sounded a big deal, until he'd come to try it. It was only once he'd made a start that he realised all the implications. He knew he couldn't go through with it. He felt incredibly guilty about even attempting the scam, and prayed that there was no trace left of his aborted intervention. The only problem he had was how to tell the boss.

As it turned out, he didn't have to.

When nothing had happened, two men had come to see him. He had desperately tried to explain to them that it was impossible to do what the boss wanted, but they had turned very nasty and said he would regret his decision. He had almost confessed the whole thing to Carolyn, but really didn't want to admit to his stupidity. He was getting more and more scared. In fact, terrified would be a more accurate description.

It was just before the wedding . . . literally. They stopped him on the street outside the church and told him that they would seriously damage Carolyn, if not actually kill her. When he saw them, he'd decided he had no choice but to run for it. They made sure he'd seen they were carrying guns, and suddenly he realised they'd meant everything they said.

Now, sat in his car, Henry was at a loss. At some point, he needed to decide what to do. He'd almost contacted his fiancée several times since yesterday's awful events, but, not knowing what to say, had left it. Henry knew Carolyn would be safer without him around right now — but surely the boss couldn't keep searching for him forever? Though even when all this died down, how could Carolyn ever forgive him? He knew she'd never understand. She was much too honest.

On reflection, he didn't know why he'd even been tempted to commit the fraud. He sat in his car, thinking about the events of the past few weeks that had culminated in the aborted wedding. Tears filled his eyes. He should have been in the Seychelles by now, happily married and looking forward to his future. Instead, he was living amongst all the rubbish of his life, packed into a car. He fervently hoped that he was now safe and that Carolyn would someday be able to forgive him. Who could tell — one day perhaps they might even get together again.

He looked out at the wonderful scenery of Cornwall. It meant nothing to him. Hills and valleys, streams and flowers. They were all around him, but he could barely see them. What on earth was he going to do next? He'd driven there in desperation after leaving their home. It was far enough away to give him time to think. Everyone at his office had expected him to be away on honeymoon for two weeks, so he knew he'd be safe for a while. He'd actually done nothing wrong. Maybe he should come clean and tell the heads of the company, and if they fired him, so be it. He deserved it.

For the umpteenth time he thought of going back, and then changed his mind. Scared of being tracked, he'd decided to turn his mobile off and leave it off. He knew the boss had his number. He didn't know how he'd obtained it, but he had, and was probably capable of tracking him.

He sat there, wondering what on earth to do next. His money would run out quite soon. He didn't even want to withdraw any cash or use his credit cards, in case of being followed.

'Oh Carolyn,' he murmured. 'I'm so sorry. Really sorry. Can you ever forgive me?'

★ ★ ★

After staying with her brother for a couple of days, Carolyn felt she'd had enough. His girlfriend Mel was due back home again and she didn't want to be in their way.

'I think I should go home, Paul. You've been wonderful, but I need to get used to the single life again. I'll be fine now. I'm over the worst. Really.'

'I don't think you should go just yet. I mean, what will you do all day?'

'I could always go back to work.'

'It's much too soon. They'll all want to ask you questions. What happened, how you are, all that. Stay here a bit longer.'

'You need your space back,' she argued. 'And you need to go back to work. They won't be happy with you if you take more time off. I'll go back home this afternoon.'

Paul gave a shrug. He knew better than to try to persuade his sister to do something against her will. 'Okay, if you think you're ready. But promise me you'll phone me every day, morning and evening. I need to know you're still standing.'

She agreed and began to pack up her things.

'I'd better run you back. Your car is still at the flat, isn't it?' She nodded. 'I'll make us some lunch and then we'll go back to your place. You'll need some shopping, too.'

'However did you get to be so organised?'

'Comes naturally, of course. I hope you really are all right. I'll go and see what there is to eat.'

He produced a quick lunch of bread and cheese and some salad. Carolyn couldn't help but smile at him. 'Thanks so much for looking after me,' she said warmly. 'You've been amazing. And I do admire your housekeeping. Mum would have been proud of you.'

'Aw, shucks,' Paul replied, adopting a dreadful American twang. 'Ya shouldn't flatter me so.'

Carolyn smiled at him and clutched his hand, feeling her tears start to flow again.

'Hey, come on now. Are you really sure you want to go home?'

'Yes of course,' she sniffed. 'It's just when people are nice to me . . . I'll go back to work in a couple of days. That'll keep my mind occupied.'

'But people might just be nice to you there. If you cry when that happens . . . '

'I'll be fine. Give me a couple of days and I can cope with anything. When do you expect Mel back?'

'Not sure. Probably not till later tonight. So I'll have plenty of time to install you back at your place and do some food shopping on our way.'

★   ★   ★

They stood in the supermarket. Paul was trying to persuade his sister to think about meals and what she might need, but Carolyn just stared at the items he was picking out. In desperation, he shoved several tins and things for the freezer into the trolley, then added fresh fruit and vegetables and continued towards the checkout. 'Oh, have you got tea and coffee at home?'

'I don't know. Probably,' Carolyn muttered.

'I'll pick some up. And milk and bread. You must have stuff to spread on it.'

'Probably.'

'Come on, Carolyn. Face up to it: you're on your own again, and you need to get your life back on track. Or come back with me and stay with us.'

'I'm so sorry. You're right, of course. I need to get myself together. Right, I'll have some marmalade and cheese. I can make cheese on toast for supper.'

'No, you won't. You'll cook something sensible. I've put a fish pie in the trolley. You should have that.'

'You always did like to boss me around, didn't you?'

'You need looking after. Who else will do it if I don't?'

She paid with her credit card and they drove back to her flat. It really was just hers now. She'd bought it with money left to her by her parents, and Henry had moved in with her. This was about to be the first time she'd ever lived there on her own. It would be very strange not waiting for Henry to come in from work. Often she was home first and usually put some dinner together ready for when he came in. Now it was a single meal and she could eat whenever she wanted to. She hated the whole idea.

Paul went inside first. There were several letters on the mat and Carolyn glanced at them. 'I can't read them now,' she said.

He carried the shopping into the kitchen and put stuff away in the fridge and freezer. Carolyn was sitting in the main room, looking rather miserable. He was reaching the end of his tether with her, but maintained his patience a while longer. When he went into the bedroom and saw the wedding dress dumped on the floor, he picked it up, remembering her excitement as they rode in the taxi to the church.

'You bastard, Henry,' he murmured. 'Why on earth did you do it?' He put the dress into a bag and stuffed it into the back of the wardrobe, then decided it would be better to take it back to his place. Out of sight, out of mind, he thought. He straightened the bed covers and went back into the lounge.

'Right, I've put the shopping away and put your bag on the bed. I'll leave you to unpack. You sure you'll be all right?'

'One day, maybe,' Carolyn replied enigmatically, then shook her head and said in a stronger voice, 'Yes. I'll be fine. You go back home now. Get ready for Mel's return. Don't worry about me. I'll work things out.'

'Okay, then. I'll be off now, and I'll call you later.'

'Thank you so much for everything, Paul. Especially for being my brother. Everyone should have one.'

He took her in his arms and gave her a big hug, then wiped away the tears that were forming in her eyes. 'I'm happy to be here for you. Let's face it, we've needed each other for a few years now. Since the parents left us, it's been down to us to stay together.'

'You do more for me than I do for you. I'm sorry.'

'Hey, you're my kid sister. You'd barely finished university when they went. You've come a long way since then.'

The dreadful car accident had devastated both of them at the time. Their parents had been travelling along a motorway when a lorry had lost control and crushed their car. They had both been killed instantly. Paul and Carolyn had stood side by side at their funeral, lost, and wondering how they'd ever cope. It had all happened over five years ago, and they had come to terms with it all and moved on. At least their parents had left them enough money to buy their own places, with some left over.

'You're right,' Carolyn said. 'We got through that, so I know I'll come to terms with the loss of Henry. Just a feeling a bit raw at the moment.'

'I know you'll be all right. I'll call you later. Bye, now.'

'Bye, and thanks again.'

Carolyn forced herself to go into the bedroom. She had expected to see her discarded wedding dress lying on the floor. She rushed to the wardrobe and saw it had gone. Paul must have taken it. Perhaps it was just as well. She wasn't really sure she wanted to see it ever again.

Sadly, she unpacked the bag she'd taken to Paul's and looked at her honeymoon case. Taking a deep breath, she opened it and began to take out all her lovely things. She laid them all on the bed, trying to decide where she would put them permanently. There was plenty of storage space, especially now that Henry's stuff had gone. Wiping away her tears, the ones that seemed to have filled her eyes yet again, she stuffed it all in various drawers, deciding to leave it there for however long it took.

She drew in another deep breath and went through to the kitchen, where she put on the kettle to make herself some coffee. *I'll get over this*, she told herself. She was determined.

3

It was a month since the day that Henry had let her down. Carolyn tried to hate him, but she couldn't. Ever since her return home, she found herself making excuses for his behaviour. She hadn't even mentioned his name to her work colleagues after she had returned to the office. Everyone was treating her differently and they all seemed to want to sympathise. She had finally stood up in the middle of the office and made a speech.

'I know you're all sorry for me and want to help me. Henry's gone. I don't know where, but it would really help me if you treated me normally and didn't look at me as if I'm about to burst into tears. I might cry sometimes, but please, I beg you, just let me shed my tears. I don't need anyone to fuss over me. Thank you all.'

There had been a slight murmuring amongst her friends, and then someone had started to clap. Soon they had all begun to join in, and that was it. Since that moment, they'd been treating her just as they always had done, and she managed to work properly and get on with her life. Several of her girlfriends had asked her to join them for a drink after work, and she'd even been to the theatre with some of them. Her words had the effect she'd hoped for, and she was beginning to think she was really starting a new life. Only a month.

Paul had let her off phoning him twice a day and was content with her occasional calls. He had been inviting her to join them for a meal on Sundays but she had declined, preferring to stay alone and cook something simple for herself. Mind you, she was getting sick of scrambled eggs and cheese on toast, and planned to make more of an effort at some point in the future.

It was a Saturday afternoon. The phone rang and Paul invited her to come over for a barbeque. 'I'll be okay,' she said at first.

'Rubbish, Carolyn. Get into your car and get yourself over here. We've got several friends coming round and they all know about your situation, and have promised not to say a word.'

'Okay. Thanks. What time?'

'Come now. You can help prepare the salads.'

'On my way,' she said with a smile. She went to change into something reasonably suitable for a barbeque and set off. She stopped at the supermarket on her way past and bought some wine.

When she arrived at her brother's, she wondered where she should park. There were several cars outside their cottage, so she left hers some way along the road. As she walked to the door, she wondered who would be there. She knew many of Paul's friends. She brushed a stray hair out of her eyes and knocked on the door.

'Hi there,' said Paul cheerfully. 'Come on in. Everyone's come early, so the party's already started.'

'I brought some wine,' she told him, then gasped in surprise. 'But I left it in the car — sorry!'

'No worries. There's plenty here. We can always get it when we've run out.'

'Carolyn, lovely to see you,' Mel said, running from the kitchen to give her a hug. 'You're just in time to give me a hand with some of the salads. If you don't mind, that is.'

'Course not. Gives me a purpose in life.'

'Come on. Paul's been concentrating on getting the barbeque started, and that seems to take all his time. Typical male, isn't he?'

Carolyn smiled and followed her to the kitchen. Soon they were carrying out large bowls of salad and she had to face the crowd.

'Hi, Carolyn — good to see you.' She was embraced by Jack, an old friend of her brother's. 'I think you know Katie, and that's Dave and Tracey over there.'

'Hi, everyone. Good to see you

again.' In truth, she didn't even know who a couple of them were, but it didn't seem to matter. They welcomed her into the group and soon she was sitting with a glass of wine in her hand. Paul went inside and came back with a man she hadn't seen before.

'Hi, everyone. This is Jed, a friend of mine. Make him welcome, please. There's a space next to my sister, Carolyn. Shove up, sis, and make some more space. I'll get you some wine, Jed.'

'Sorry, I didn't mean to squish you like that,' Jed said to Carolyn as he squeezed in beside her.

'No worries. I should have made more room for you. Are you okay there?'

'Fine. Oh thanks, Paul,' he said as he was handed some wine.

'Can I top you up?' Paul asked his sister.

'I mustn't drink too much or I won't be able to drive home,' she replied.

'You can always stay over. Come on, drink up.'

She accepted a refill and sat back, ready to enjoy herself. Jed seemed nice. He was certainly a good-looking bloke and seemed to chat easily. She wondered why she'd never met him before and why Paul had never mentioned him.

'So, how do you know Paul?' she asked him.

'We used to play rugger together for a time. Then I moved to Cornwall and we sort of lost touch. I was coming to see my parents and wanted to see him. So, here I am.'

'So what do you do?'

'I'm a freelance photographer. Local papers, magazines, and so on. Makes me a living, and I adore Cornwall. It's so beautiful. Do you know it?'

'Not really. We went to St Ives for a holiday when I was small. I think Paul and Mel have been back a few times, though.'

'You should come and visit again.'

'I'll think about it.' She took a sip of her wine. 'I take it you're not married?'

'Me? No. Think I'm allergic the whole idea of marriage. How about you?'

Carolyn gulped. She'd assumed they all knew about her recent loss. 'No, I'm not married,' she managed to say without shedding a tear.

'Good. That's a start, then. Not attached in any way?'

'No, no attachments.' She couldn't help but feel guilty as she said this, but she stuck to it and didn't even blush.

'And what do you do?'

'I work for a company specialising in interior home design,' she said, and started to tell him a little more about what she did.

'Here we go,' Paul said as he placed a large platter full of cooked meat on the table. Everyone complimented him and reached out to fill their plates. 'There's cutlery in the middle — and Mel, can you put the salads on the table? It'll be easier if everyone stays where they are.'

Mel carried several bowls over and put them onto the table. Luckily it was a large one and there was plenty of room. It actually felt good, Carolyn realised, to be sitting out in their tiny garden with friends. She smiled at Paul and winked at him. He smiled back at her and filled his own plate.

'Here's to the cooks,' said Jack, raising his glass. 'Oops, I'm sorry, but I've run out of wine. Must have been Tracey who drank it,' he said with good humour.

'I beg your pardon,' protested Tracey. 'It was you, you greedy thing.'

'Was it? Sorry. Pass the bottle over here, someone, before I die of thirst.'

When all the food had been eaten and everyone vowed they'd never eat again, they cleared the empty dishes away, and some of the guests went into the kitchen to wash up despite Mel's protestations.

'You don't have to do this, really,' she insisted. 'I'll do it with Paul later.'

'We're doing it, so shut up,' said one with a smile. 'Besides, it gives us a chance to catch up with all the gossip.'

Carolyn blushed and felt suddenly weak. She made some excuse to go upstairs, and when she came back they'd all more or less finished.

'You all right, love?' asked Mel kindly.

'Fine. Sorry, I needed the loo.'

'Don't worry, they didn't mention you at all. I take it you haven't heard anything from Henry?'

'Not a thing. I'm not even thinking of him anymore. I just get angry when I do.'

'Good for you. Jed's nice, don't you think?'

'I suppose he is. Hadn't really thought about it. He lives in Cornwall anyway, so he isn't much use as a long-term relationship prospect,' she said with a laugh.

'He and Paul were very good friends when we first met. Inseparable, they were — and then he went off to live in the wilds.'

'Where do you keep this dish?' Carolyn asked as she finished drying it.

40

'I'll take it. Have to admit, it usually stays in the spare room under the bed. It's too big to go in the cupboards! Now, let's get another drink. You are staying, I presume?'

'Well, thanks. If I have another drink, I may need to.'

The evening wore on, and they all moved inside the small lounge room as it got cooler. Jed sat close to Carolyn for most of the time and seemed to enjoy her company. She felt guilty but gradually relaxed — until she felt his arm rest gently across the top of her shoulders. She stiffened but couldn't find the words to tell him to stop. Instead, she moved away.

'Sorry,' she mumbled, and ran upstairs into one of the bedrooms.

Paul followed her. 'Are you OK?' he asked as he stepped inside.

'Yes. I'm sorry. It was just a bit unexpected.'

'Come on. He won't do it again, I'm sure.'

She followed him downstairs and

went to sit next to Jed. He smiled at her and apologised quietly. Eventually, the rest of the group decided to call it a day and went off home, leaving just Carolyn and Jed with Paul and Mel. They talked for a while until Carolyn said she was almost falling asleep and must go to bed.

'Will you be all right on the sofa, Jed?' Paul asked him. 'It's reasonably long, so you won't be too cramped.'

'I'll be fine. It's very good of you to put me up at all.'

'Purely selfish, of course. Gives us tomorrow to really talk again. We need to catch up on the past few years. Mel, have we got a duvet or something?'

She went upstairs and came down with a duvet and pillow. Then they went up to bed and left Jed and Carolyn downstairs.

'I am so sorry about before,' Jed apologised again.

'I was dumped at the altar,' said Carolyn, surprising herself with her sudden explanation. 'No warning. Nothing. Takes a lot to get over it, but I'm getting there. I'm sorry, too, that I reacted the way I did. It's not that I don't like you. It's just that it wasn't all that long ago, and I'm nowhere near ready to think about . . . anyone else.'

Jed looked at her with empathy in his eyes, and nodded. 'I lost my girlfriend. Gosh, that sounds somewhat careless,' he added wryly. 'She went off with another man and left me alone. I moved to Cornwall as a sort of escape. It was a couple of years ago. I've made a life there now, and though I feel lonely at times, it's a good place to be.'

'I'm sorry. That kind of betrayal isn't easy to get past.'

'About earlier on . . . it was presumptuous of me.'

'It's fine. I'm glad we understand a little more about each other now. And now I really must go to bed before I fall asleep where I stand.' To her own surprise, she stood on tiptoe and kissed him lightly on his cheek. 'Nightie night.'

He looked surprised too, and touched where she'd kissed him. 'Night,' Jed whispered, watching her go upstairs.

He felt very attracted to Carolyn. Could there be any future for them? There was no telling, but he knew he wanted to get to know her better.

He settled down to sleep, but it was a long time coming. He'd driven all the way there in one go and still felt the hum of the wheels somewhere in the depths of his body. He was planning to stay for a few days at least, and now he hoped he would get to see much more of his friend's sister.

*   *   *

Carolyn fell asleep quite quickly but she woke early. She was desperate for some tea but knew she couldn't go and make it without disturbing Jed. The stairs led down into the lounge, where he was sleeping. She lay there, reflecting on the evening. It had been fun, and she had to admit to enjoying chatting to Paul

44

and Mel's friends. Nobody had said a word to her about Henry, and that felt good. She still missed him like crazy, and still wondered where he was and why he had never got in touch with her. She longed for him to come into the flat with his usual cheery 'hi there' resonating. The thought caused tears to prick at her eyes, and she blinked them away. No more tears, she had vowed.

She heard movement and sat up. Someone knocked at her door. 'Come in,' she called.

'Hope you don't mind — I made some tea and brought it up.' Jed looked ruffled and, wearing only a singlet and shorts, also very attractive.

'You must be a mind-reader. I was wondering if I might creep past you to make some. Here, sit down on the bed.' She took the mug from him and he sat beside her.

'I think Mel and Paul are both still in dreamland,' he said. 'No sounds from them, anyway. So, how did you sleep?'

'Quite well, actually. You?'

'Not a lot. I was thinking about you and all the chaos that you've been through. I really do feel for you.'

'Thanks, but I'm not allowing myself to think about it anymore. He's gone. Four years obviously meant less to him than it did to me, so that's that.'

'Well said. You're very lovely, and you certainly won't find it hard to find someone else.'

'Well thank you. But I'm not sure I'll ever want anyone else. Once bitten, and all that.'

'Then I'll have to set about changing your views. How about coming out to lunch with me? It's okay, I'll invite Paul and Mel too,' he clarified, noticing her slight look of panic at his suggestion.

'I really ought to go back home. I only left for an evening.'

'What do you have to do? Have you left the cooker on or something? Left the fridge defrosting?'

She giggled. 'Nothing like that.'

He grinned at her and slowly she smiled back.

'Okay,' she said, 'lunch it is. But we'll go Dutch — I insist.'

'Well that won't work, as I want to treat Paul and Mel. You might as well just accept it.'

'Persistent, aren't you? Okay, thanks. Might have to go back to my flat to change though.'

'And I suppose I should go and get dressed before Paul thinks I'm up to no good. Not that I'd mind, of course, but I'd hate for your reputation to be damaged.'

'It doesn't really look good to have you sitting on my bed half-undressed — despite the provision of tea, of course. And for your future information, I don't usually drink it with milk.'

'Most promising thing I've heard all morning. Suggests you might allow me to make tea for you again.'

He left her to get dressed, and went downstairs. He felt happy after their light-hearted conversation. Clearly it was all a bit soon for her, but maybe in the future they might have a chance

— although he was determined not to hurry things. Carolyn was clearly still reeling.

She came downstairs when she was dressed and found Jed sitting reading the paper. 'Do you want some breakfast?' she asked.

'Will they mind? It isn't exactly our kitchen, is it?'

'Paul's my brother. He won't mind at all. Don't forget, I stayed here for ages. Well, a couple of days, anyway. I'll make some toast and see what there is to put on it. It's all right, you stay there. You can tell me what's going on in the big wide world.'

'I was looking at some of the pictures they've used, actually. One or two are really good, but several of them are far and away from decent.'

'How good are you? I mean, if you don't rate these pictures . . . '

'Oh I suppose I'm not brilliant,' Jed said with a shrug. 'It's just frustration talking. Some of the angles are pretty suspect, and I think there's more of a story there somewhere. Forget it. It's just me sounding off.'

Carolyn went in search of bread to make toast. She put four slices into the toaster and put the kettle on. 'More tea?' she called to him.

'Please. I'll come through.'

'It's all right. There's not exactly a lot of space in here.'

'That's fine with me.'

Carolyn shivered. He was certainly attractive, and was making no bones about fancying her. She felt embarrassed. If things had gone to plan, she would have been a married woman by now, and she would never, ever have been even looking at anyone else.

'Jed,' she began, 'I'm a bit . . . ' She was going to say 'vulnerable' or 'delicate', but she stopped.

'I know. I understand about Henry and what you went through, so no worries there. Trouble is, I really like you, and I'm only here for a short time, so I need to make a good impression on you! Oops — watch out, the toast is about to burst into flames,' he said, reaching round her to press the button. He brushed her bare arms as he did so, and she felt a strange sort of tremor run through her. It was ridiculous. She hardly knew him, so put it down to her vulnerable state. She was, after all, feeling rather sensitive.

'I think it's still edible, just about,' he commented.

'Sorry. I'm not good in the kitchen. Henry was always complaining about my lack of ability.'

'Then Henry was rather silly. It was just because I was talking to you that the toast nearly burnt. Have you found anything to spread on it?' he asked.

'Should be something in the cupboard over the sink.'

He reached into the cupboard and produced a range of jams and marmalade and also a pot of honey. She set out two plates and put the toast onto them. Everything she was doing seemed to be in slow motion, as if she was thinking hard about her actions. Absent-mindedly, she spread butter on all the slices, and started to add marmalade.

'Whoa there. I don't like marmalade,' Jed told her. 'Jam or honey for me.'

'Sorry. I wasn't thinking.'

'Strikes me you were thinking a bit too much. Here, give me my plate. I'll do the rest. You go and sit down and I'll bring the tea in to you.'

'Thanks,' she said. 'I think I must be hungover.'

4

The two of them seemed to find plenty to talk about. They went to sit out in the small garden and enjoy the summer sunshine. It was well after eleven o'clock before Paul and Mel came down.

'Hello, you two,' Mel said. 'I hope you found some breakfast. Sorry we're so late. Only just woke up. My last day of rest before I go back to work in the morning. Well, later tonight, actually.' Her job as a flight attendant entailed rather erratic hours, and often she had to leave home in the middle of the night.

'Where are you going this time?' Carolyn asked.

'Long haul to Australia,' she replied. 'I'll be away for a week or so.'

'However do you cope, Paul?' asked Jed.

'Oh it gives me space to enjoy life,' he teased.

'Watch it, you,' Mel retorted. 'I'll leave you a list of things to do while I'm away.'

'Don't worry, I've got heaps to do,' Paul said. 'Looking after this character, for one thing. You're staying till next weekend, aren't you, Jed?'

'I hope so. I'd quite like to do a bit of work around here. Some moody shots of life in a city.'

'Hardly a city! I've got a couple of days off too, so maybe we can do something then.'

'Great. What are you doing, Carolyn?'

'Working, of course,' she replied.

'Can't you get some time off too? Be good to all go out together.'

'I dunno. Maybe later in the week.'

'I'm off tomorrow and Tuesday,' Paul told her. 'Couldn't you get time off then?'

'I'm not like you, Paul. I can't just get time off whenever I want it. Maybe

I could get Thursday off; not before then, though.'

'Well that's a date, then,' Jed said. 'The three of us can go out together, then Paul can leave us alone and we'll go somewhere nice on our own. Now, everyone, are you ready to go out for lunch? On me, of course.'

'There's no need for that,' Paul said.

'I want to. Least I can do. I'm going to take Carolyn home to get changed and we'll come back to pick you up.'

'That's all right, I've got my car parked down the road — I'll go and change and meet you there,' she said.

'Go on then, shoo.' Jed gave her a smile. 'Go and get glammed up, ready for the meal of your life.'

Carolyn giggled and got up from her seat, went upstairs and collected her jacket and handbag, then came back down and said her goodbyes. She set off along the road to where she had left her car.

When she got there, she was taken aback. She could have sworn she'd left her car along here, but there was no sign of it. She turned and went the other way, but it had obviously gone. Disappeared. Who on earth would want to steal it? It was hardly a new model, and a rather boring one anyway, she thought. She went back into Paul's place.

'My car — it's gone! It must have been stolen.'

'No!' her brother gasped. 'How awful! Where did you leave it?'

'Along the road. Not all that near. I never thought about it; just stopped in the first available space. Oh heavens, what should I do?'

'I'll call the police,' said Paul firmly. 'Don't worry, love. Possibly they've found it already. Joy-riders, I expect.' He went back inside and Carolyn could hear him talking on the phone. When he returned, he said, 'I'll take you home, if you really need to go and change. Though you'll do fine as you are.'

'I can't even contemplate going out

for lunch. Sorry, but I need to get this sorted first. What shall I do if they haven't found it?'

Everyone was sympathetic and made various suggestions, including Jed offering to take and fetch her from work. She explained that she needed her car for visiting clients, so she might need to hire one. Paul said the police had told him they'd keep a lookout for hers, and had provided him with a report number.

'What use is that?' Carolyn asked angrily.

'So you can report the theft to your insurance company,' Paul explained. 'Have you got your details with you?'

'I don't know.'

'You're supposed to carry your insurance certificate whenever you drive the car. Don't tell me you left it there.'

'No, I didn't.'

Finally they agreed that they would all go with Carolyn to her flat and sort the matter out from there. Carolyn went with Jed in his car, while Paul took Mel in his.

'Don't worry too much,' Jed said to Carolyn on the way. 'I'll be here to drive you wherever you need to go.'

'Thanks, that's good of you. But it's your holiday and I don't want to spoil it.'

'It's really not a problem. I like being around you.'

She looked at him thoughtfully, then said, 'Turn left here. There are usually plenty of parking spaces.'

They parked outside her flat in the dedicated parking area. Jed locked his car and followed her upstairs. He looked round appreciatively. 'This is nice,' he told her. 'You've furnished it beautifully. Just right. Minimalist, but still comfortable and homely.'

'I should hope so. It is my job, after all. Not that I get many places like this to design for. Our clients are usually very wealthy and want gold trimmings on everything.'

'Now that must be tough.'

'Not really. I just pander to their wishes and suggest a few changes. Now, I must look for my insurance stuff. Excuse me.' She went to her desk and started to look through her various files. She pulled out her insurance documents and found the number to call, then gave them the details and the report number provided by the police. The insurance agent told her she should wait for a day, and if her car had not been found by then she could hire a similar-sized car.

'But what do I do in the meantime?' Carolyn said as she put the phone down. 'I need my car for work. Damn them! Looks as though I'll have to take tomorrow off after all.'

'Excellent,' Jed said. 'I think the others are here. Shall I let them in?'

Once Paul and Mel were inside, they all discussed what should happen next, and decided they still wanted to go to the pub for lunch.

'The police have your mobile number, so if they hear anything, they'll call you,'

Paul said to his sister. 'So come on, let's go and eat.'

Somewhat unwillingly, Carolyn agreed, though she still felt very worried and hoped she'd get her car back in one piece.

★　★　★

They were eating pudding when Carolyn's phone rang. It was the police to say they'd found a burnt-out wreck of a car similar to hers. She went white and slumped back heavily.

'When will you know if it's mine?' She listened for a while. 'It does sound like mine. Is there nothing left to identify it positively? I see. Well, thank you.' She switched off her phone. 'Looks as though I'm buying a new car,' she announced.

'Oh, rotten luck,' Jed said. 'What did they say?'

She told them, and they were all sympathetic. 'I'll need to hire something while I look,' she said. 'Not sure if the insurance will pay for it or not.'

'Leave it for a day or two and take up my offer,' Jed suggested.

'I can't. Thanks a lot, but I do need to be independent. I need to be able to manage on my own.'

'Sis, Jed won't mind,' Paul told her. 'In fact, I suspect he'd quite relish the idea of running you round.'

'It's still too soon,' she muttered.

'I'm only offering to drive you, not marry you,' Jed replied.

'How can I accept when you say things like that?'

Paul was laughing and so was Mel. 'Methinks the lady doth protest too much,' he said.

'What? What do you mean by that remark?'

'Nothing, dear sister. Nothing at all. Stop being so prickly. Now, are we having coffee?'

Carolyn sat fuming. She felt none of them were taking her predicament seriously. She drank the coffee that someone had ordered, feeling as if she were in the middle of a nightmare. Perhaps she would wake up any moment now and everything would be all right. Her beloved little car would be there, parked in its usual place. But she knew it wasn't a dream. She would be forced to search out a new car. The old one had held such sentimental value for her. She and Henry had bought it together about three years ago to celebrate her new promotion. She felt tears burning at her eyes.

'What do you think?' someone was asking her. She gave a start.

'Sorry? Think about what?'

'We're thinking of taking a walk over the Downs Banks,' Paul said.

'Oh, you go if you want to. Leave me out of it.'

'So what will you do instead? Sit and fret about your lack of a car? Or maybe you'll sit and while away the afternoon crying again.' Paul knew her all too well. What else would she do?

'All right,' she agreed. 'Downs Banks it is.'

They all enjoyed their walk in the warm sunshine, and there was a lot of laughter and joking. Carolyn began to think there might indeed be a new life awaiting her. Jed even took her hand at one point, and she didn't pull away. That was certainly progress, she decided. It felt good to hold his hand, and it wasn't actually committing her to anything, was it?

After their walk, they went back to Carolyn's flat and she made tea. 'Sorry,' she apologised, 'but I haven't got anything to feed you all on.'

'Personally, I'm still full after lunch,' Mel replied. 'It shouldn't be too long before we need to go, Paul. I've got to pack and I need to get some sleep. Or maybe Jed would like to stay here with you for a while yet? I don't mind going on my own, if Jed can bring you back home with him.'

'It's okay, I'll come with you,' Paul told her. 'Can't have you going off without me, and well, I'd like to be there to say goodbye. I'll give Jed my key so he can let himself back in whenever he chooses. Okay with you guys?'

'Fine by me,' Jed told them. 'I'm sure Carolyn won't mind putting up with me for a while longer.'

'Well, no, although I do have some stuff to get ready for work tomorrow,' she said.

'I can help. My skills aren't limited to photography, you realise. I can set things up to make a good impression.'

'Oh it's nothing like that. I just need to check my briefcase and sort out what I'm going to wear. General stuff like that. Won't take me long.'

'And I'm going to be your chauffeur for the day,' Jed reminded her.

'Well, you can take me to work, thanks. If you're sure it won't put you out too much?'

'Are you ready to head off?' Paul asked Mel.

'I think so. Thanks for the tea, Carolyn. It's so nice to see you joining in with life again. Take care, love.' They hugged. 'And I'll say bye to you too, Jed, just in case I don't see you before I go.'

'Bye, Mel, and thanks for putting me up,' he said. 'I'll see you next time. Have a good trip.' Then they were gone, and Jed was alone with Carolyn.

'Well, here we are,' he said with a smile. 'What would you like to do with what's left of today?'

'I haven't really thought about it. Anything you want to do?'

'To be honest, I usually slump in front of the television on Sunday evenings. Calm before the storm of Monday morning.'

'That's pretty much what I do too. Do you mind if I go and change?'

'Course I don't mind. It's a very nice shirt, though. Such a pretty blue. Makes your eyes look ... well, I suppose they are brown, but at times they look sort of dark blue. Bluey-brown-eyed blond. Quite an unusual combination.'

'Nice of you to say so. You've got

brown eyes, too. Quite a dark brown.'

'I hope you approve?'

'Course. Henry was quite blond. Well, he probably still is.'

'You haven't heard anything from him?'

'No, nothing. Sorry, I shouldn't be talking about him, to you of all people.'

'I don't mind. Tell me about it all, and then I won't put my foot in it.'

So she began to tell him. She felt quite unemotional and, for the first time, could speak about it in a quite matter-of-fact way. 'He was acting a bit odd just before the wedding. When I think about it, his behaviour was rather odd the whole week before. I reckon something must have happened. Something to upset him. But he left, and as far as I'm concerned, I obviously meant little enough to him.'

'I'm sorry. You don't deserve to be treated like that. I can't imagine what he thought he was doing.'

'Believe me, neither can I. I've thought it through time and time again and still ended up with zero. But, enough of me. Tell me about what happened with you.'

'Not a lot to tell,' Jed sighed. 'I had a fiancée who decided she didn't want to know, and left me for someone else. She's now happily married and expecting her second child. I went down to Cornwall to find work and a complete change of lifestyle. It really suits me down there. You should come down to visit. I bet it'll catch you and fill your senses as it did mine. It's such a wonderful place to live. Fresh air and gorgeous views. I'll show you some pictures. I'm assuming you haven't been again since you were little?'

'We did go that way once more. Might have been Devon, actually.'

'It's quite different there. Still lovely of course, but different. I do go to take pictures there sometimes. Always feel I'm going home when I return. I've got a cottage quite close to the sea. Well, I say next to the sea, but it's some way above. It's got some amazing views, especially when the trees don't have leaves.'

'You're quite a salesman. I'll certainly have to come and see it for myself.'

Jed beamed at her. 'Good. When might that be?'

'Oh, I don't know. One day maybe.'

'How about coming back with me next week?'

'Next week? Oh, I couldn't possibly.'

'Why not?'

She tried hard to think of reasons and fell back on her workload. Actually, it wasn't all that bad at the moment. She'd cleared most of her stuff before their aborted honeymoon and had been merely keeping up with things since then. Besides, it was their quiet time of year, when many folks were on holiday. A little break in Cornwall might be rather nice. But she couldn't possibly stay with Jed.

'Come on, why not?' Jed repeated. 'I've got a spare room, so you'd be quite safe,' he added with a grin.

'Let me think about it. And thank

you, you're very kind. I'm not sure about staying with you, though. Spare room or no, I'm not sure it would be quite right.'

'Oh for goodness' sake. This is the twenty-first century. And I'm not going to pounce on you during the night!'

'I need to look at my work diary. Chat to my boss, etcetera. I've also got to sort out my transport, don't forget.'

'I'll drive you both ways,' he offered. 'Not a problem. It would be great to show you Cornwall. I just know you'll love it.'

'We'll see. You're very generous.'

They spent a happy, rather lazy evening watching television. Carolyn put together a simple supper and they ate from trays, still watching. Just after ten o'clock, Jed rose and decided to leave for Paul's.

'I'd better go now before I fall asleep. I'd hate to offend your moral principles by sleeping on your sofa.'

She smiled, wondering if she should offer him a bed for the night. But she decided against it. Well, he didn't have a toothbrush. It was important that everyone should have access to a toothbrush, she decided.

'What time do you need me tomorrow morning?' he asked her.

'If you're really sure . . . I need to be at work by nine thirty, so can you be here at nine?'

'Not a problem. I'll see you then. Sleep well.' He kissed her perfunctorily on the cheek and breezed out. 'See you in the morning.'

She leaned against the door when he had gone. Her mind was racing around the possibilities of leaving here the following week. What would everyone think? Cornwall was a long way to go. Suppose they didn't get on and it all went pear-shaped? She'd be stuck there, without a car or any means of getting home again. And Jed might have to work. How would she feel about being left alone all day, with nowhere to go?

No, it was a foolish idea. She would

tell him so the next morning. He was very kind and would undoubtedly put himself out considerably to accommodate her, but she really felt it wouldn't be right. One day, perhaps — one day in her uncertain future she would go and stay somewhere and look him up. That would be quite enough, wouldn't it?

She went to bed and lay there for some time, wide awake, her brain racing round in circles. She even felt slightly guilty for enjoying life without Henry. What was he doing? She hoped he was all right. Whatever he'd put her through, she still felt some affection for him. It was a different feeling to forgiving him. That, she didn't think she would ever be able to do. But the memories of the fun they'd had, the good times they'd spent, all meant something to her.

At last she fell asleep, and woke slightly late the next day.

★ ★ ★

Jed rang her doorbell promptly at nine o'clock. She let him in and said she'd be a minute or two.

'No worries,' he said easily. 'Did you sleep well?'

'Bit mixed,' she told him. 'I was too busy thinking.'

'About Cornwall, I hope.'

'That *is* what I've been thinking about. But, Jed, I don't think it's such a good idea. I mean, even if I can get time off work, I'd hate to be stuck somewhere without my car.'

'You could always use mine. I have a motorbike I sometimes use for work. Not that I have to work all the time. I've done a couple of big contracts lately, so I can take time off. Two or three weeks easily. Oh, apart from next Sunday. I do have a commitment then, but you could always come with me.'

It seemed every reason not to go had been dismissed in a breath. 'I'll think about it some more,' she said. 'Right, I'm ready. Let's go.'

When they reached Carolyn's office,

Jed parked and asked when she'd like a lift anywhere.

'I don't know yet,' she replied. 'I can't keep you sitting here all day. If I need to go anywhere, I'll borrow someone's car. I think I shall be based here most of today anyway. You go off and enjoy yourself.'

'Well, if you're sure. What time do you finish?'

'About five. But don't worry about me; I can easily get a lift home. Someone will drop me off, I'm sure.'

'I insist. I'll be here at five. Now, go and work hard so you can be free next week.'

'You're impossible,' she laughed. 'But many thanks.'

'Can I have your mobile number, in case I need it for anything?' She told him what it was and he punched it into his phone. 'Great, thanks. I'll send you a text so you'll have mine. Have a good day. Bye.'

She said goodbye to him and went inside.

'Who's the new man?' asked one of her colleagues, an older lady called Mary whose desk was next to hers.

'A friend of my brother's. My car was stolen and set on fire. It's a write-off.'

'Oh no! Whoever was responsible?'

'No idea. It was parked outside my brother's place on Saturday night and someone took it. I'm going to have to get another one.'

'I'd continue to get lifts from the hunk, if I were you,' Mary said with a grin. 'He certainly looked an improvement on . . . ' She stopped speaking at this point. Carolyn knew exactly what she had been going to say and wanted to quell her embarrassment.

'It's okay. You can mention Henry's name without me falling apart. He's in the past now.'

'Very brave of you. Now, I'd better get on. Have you got the Doreman file?'

The week had begun.

* * *

At five o'clock precisely, Jed texted to say he was outside waiting for her. Carolyn texted him back to say she would be ten more minutes, and that she could get a lift if he didn't want to wait. Naturally, he did want to wait.

As she came out of the office, he stepped out of his car. 'Hi there. Good day?'

'Hello. Yes, thanks. You?'

'Not bad. I told Paul we'd meet him later. I hope that's okay with you? He's on his own this week, Mel being away.'

'Yes, of course. But if you blokes want to do something together, just the two of you, don't worry about me. I'm used to being on my own.'

He said nothing but simply smiled. They drove to her flat and he followed her inside. 'I assumed you'd want to change before we go bowling,' he said.

'Bowling?' Carolyn echoed in surprise.

'Indeed. We have a booking for seven thirty; then we're going to eat pizzas. Hope you approve.'

'Well, yes. But like I said, you don't have to include me in everything.'

'Of course we do. I want you to realise you're indispensable to my enjoyment of my week here. Did you organise your holiday for next week, by the way?'

'I'm still thinking about it,' she told him, lying through her back teeth. She had spoken to her boss, who had immediately agreed to her going away. Carolyn still wasn't all that convinced she should go, though. She might speak to Paul later, if she had the chance. He would know if she was being foolish or if she might enjoy it.

When they arrived at Carolyn's flat, and she let them in, Jed suggested she go and get ready. 'I want us to get there in good time and find some decent parking,' he said.

'Heavens, it's only just after six. I'll go and change. Put the kettle on, will you? I'm gasping for a cuppa.'

He did as he was bid and put two teabags into the mugs. He even remembered she drank it black. And as he made the tea, he wondered how he might convince Carolyn to come back to Cornwall with him.

5

As the week went on, Carolyn was more and more convinced she should go back to Cornwall with Jed. She had booked a week off, but didn't tell him that at first. Then, when she finally said she would go, he was ridiculously pleased and swung her round in a circle, telling her she wouldn't regret it.

'Well I really hope not,' she said, laughing and suddenly feeling quite dizzy.

'I'll be on my best behaviour, and I promise I'll look after you. Will you be able to get time off work?'

'I'm sure it'll be fine,' she said, fudging the truth somewhat. 'Also, I thought it might be a good idea to look at cars. The police told me it was definitely mine that had been burnt out. The insurance company have agreed that I can get another one.'

'Are you going for a new one, or looking for a used one?'

'Unfortunately, they won't give me enough for a brand-new one. Mine was only a couple of years old, but new models cost so much more.'

They discussed the opportunities available to her and decided to go and look at cars immediately. They drove to a nearby garage and wandered round the parking lot. A salesman came out to help them, or rather hoping to make a sale.

'I expect you're ready to close soon, aren't you?' Carolyn asked.

'We can stay here for as long as you need,' the salesman, who introduced himself as Charlie, said. 'Don't worry. I'll leave you to look around and come back in a few minutes.'

'Thank heavens for small mercies,' Carolyn muttered when he'd left them. 'I can't stand it when they hover round all the time.'

'Me neither,' Jed agreed. 'I was about to tell him to get lost.'

They looked at several of the cars, and at last Carolyn decided she couldn't face it any longer. 'I'll say I'm thinking about it. Let's go and see the salesman, and then we can go home.'

Charlie wanted them to sit down and talk about exactly what kind of car Carolyn wanted, but she and Jed said 'no, thanks' and left together.

Jed smiled at her as he drove her back to her flat. 'You're very good at not being pushed into anything, aren't you?'

'Maybe. Sometimes.'

'Well, it's something I admire about you. I was pretty pushy trying to get you to come to Cornwall, and you waited till you were good and ready to agree.'

Carolyn decided to come clean. 'I booked the week off on Tuesday morning, actually. I'd almost decided then, but thought I'd keep you waiting for a while. Don't want you getting complacent, now, do I?'

'You're coming, and that's all I could

have hoped for. I must phone my lady who comes to clean — make sure the place all spotless and ready for my esteemed guest.'

'Don't go to any trouble on my account.'

'Oh, I won't. I need to let her know when I'm coming back anyway. I thought we could set off early on Saturday, if that's okay with you?'

'How early?'

'I'd like to make it as soon after seven as you can be up.'

'Seven? Wow. I'd better pack tomorrow evening. No going out Friday, then. You can spend the evening with Paul on your own. He is your friend, after all.'

'Okay. I suppose we'll manage without you. What do you fancy doing this evening?'

'I ought to put some washing on. Then I can iron tomorrow evening.'

'Okay. I'll allow you five minutes to do that, then we'll go and collect Paul. Maybe go to a nice pub.'

When they arrived at Carolyn's flat, it

actually took her almost fifteen minutes. Jed was stomping round after her, grumbling at being kept waiting.

'Don't be so impatient,' she told him. 'I need to have everything clean before I go.'

'I do have a washing machine, and I understand one can easily buy soap powder in Cornwall. For goodness' sake, woman, come on.'

'Just a minute more. I need to get something from my room.'

'It's almost seven o'clock. Paul will think we're lost.' He was speaking to an empty space as she was, by then, upstairs.

'Right, ready,' Carolyn said as she came back down.

'I hope it won't take you this long on Saturday,' Jed said. 'I want to get on the road. We'll stop for breakfast at a place I know. Wonderful bacon baps.'

'With or without butter?'

'With butter, of course. Why do you ask?'

'Just winding you up,' she laughed.

It was a jolly evening. There was a folk singer playing at the pub, and they all joined in with the choruses. Paul had a lovely voice and thoroughly enjoyed himself. Jed's voice was also surprisingly good, and he sang with some gusto. They ate chilli and rice and drank beers. At the end of it all, they pulled up outside Carolyn's flat.

'That was such a good evening,' she said. 'Thank you both for including me. I won't invite you in, as I must sort out my washing and spread it to dry. Night, both of you.'

'Night,' Jed replied. 'I'll be round for nine in the morning. Your lift to work?' he reminded her when she looked at him blankly.

'Oh yes, of course. Thanks a lot.'

'No worries.'

'Night, Paul. When's Mel back, by the way?'

'Saturday at some ungodly hour in the morning,' he said with a laugh.

'Hope Jed doesn't get in her way. You know he's picking me up at seven?'

'Oh dear, no I didn't. It'll be a short night then, won't it?'

'It should be fine. We're going to stop for breakfast,' Jed said. 'Anyway, we'd better let this lady do her stuff. Bye for now, Carolyn.'

★   ★   ★

By the next morning, most of Carolyn's clothes were dry, and she piled them into her laundry basket. She would have a busy evening getting everything ready for her trip. She grabbed some toast and drank her tea, and was ready for Jed when he arrived. She ran down the stairs and met him outside.

'You're on time today,' he remarked.

'Practising for tomorrow. Actually, I've got a rather busy day ahead. I need to get everything sorted so my colleagues can answer any client questions that might come up.'

'All sounds very efficient. Right, let's go.'

When they arrived at her work place,

they met a lot of people standing outside. 'Hello, what's going on here?' Jed wondered aloud as he parked the car and got out.

'I don't know.' Carolyn got out and went over to the group. 'What's happening?'

'There's a fire,' said Sophie, the receptionist. 'Fire brigade are on their way. We've all only just arrived ourselves, and found it like this. The smell is terrible!'

'Oh heavens!' Carolyn exclaimed. 'I suppose we all have to stay out here till . . . Oh, here they come.'

The fire brigade arrived amid sirens and flashing blue lights. 'Who's in charge here?' one of them asked.

'I suppose that would be me,' said Emily, who, although she was indeed the boss, was rather a quiet person who preferred to let her staff make most of the decisions, especially now she was nearing retirement.

'Can you give me an idea of what's happening in there?' As he was speaking, the rest of the crew were unfurling yards of hose and getting ready to go inside.

'I really don't know,' Emily replied. 'But it seems as if the computers are all burning . . . '

'Hold, on chaps. Electrical fire.' At this point there was a huge roar, and the whole building seemed to be on fire. 'Okay, keep back, everyone.'

The windows shattered as the flames reached them. The fire crew started to do their work, and slowly the flames died back. They pushed inside and, gradually, the fire was doused. Then the chief came out to speak to the anxious group.

'I'm afraid it's looking pretty bad,' he said. 'There's nothing left. What was your business?'

'Home interior design. Have we really lost everything?' Sophie asked.

'I'm afraid so. I don't know if there was a fireproof safe?'

'Well yes, there was one in my office,' Emily said. 'It couldn't possibly have survived, though. Not in all that.'

'One of us will take a look later, once it's cooled down a bit and we can get inside. You say it seemed to be the computers that were burning — do you leave them on all the time?'

'No,' Emily said. 'At least, I don't think so.'

'Okay, I'll let the investigators know. They'll be round later. I think you might as well all go home. There's nothing you can do here.'

'What a loss,' Emily said in a small voice. She looked terribly pale.

'Are you all right?' asked Carolyn. 'You don't look very well.'

'It's just shock. I'll be fine. Now, let's leave these gentlemen to do their work.'

Jed stepped forward. 'What do you want to do?' he asked Carolyn.

'I suppose we should all go home. There isn't much to be done here. It's terrible.'

'At least you won't be missing anything when we're in Cornwall.'

'Oh I couldn't possibly leave at this

time. I'm sorry, but we shall need to reorganise everything . . . clients . . . and we'll need somewhere to work . . . '

'Excuse me,' interrupted Emily. 'You must go. There won't be anything left for anyone to do. If the discs are in the safe and usable, I can send out a blanket email to the clients to say everything's on hold. We shall undoubt-edly lose a few of them who want things done yesterday, but there's nothing to be done about that. To be honest, I'm not sure I shall even continue the business. I need time to think it through.'

'I see,' replied Carolyn. 'But you'll surely need some help?'

'Oh Carolyn, I'm not even sure how long I can go on paying all of you. I think it's best if you all have notice from now on. I'll let you know what I can pay you when the insurance claim goes through. I'm so sorry, everyone. Go home, all of you.' She turned away from the group, clearly very upset. She looked dreadful, and Carolyn was rather concerned about her.

'Emily, please sit down,' she said. 'Let's go to your car. I don't want you fainting or something. Jed, can you help me to get her to her car?'

'Emily can't possibly drive in this state,' he said quietly to her.

'I could drive her home.'

'Okay, I can follow you to bring you home too.'

The rest of the group were all talking earnestly, debating what they were going to do. They were all concerned about their boss, who, despite not being terribly dynamic, was very popular. Jed felt quite proud of Carolyn as she took over and organised things.

'Right, everyone — I'll take Emily home now. I suggest you all go home, too, and wait to see what tomorrow brings. Or Monday, should I say.'

The group left the building to its smoky demise, and one by one got into their cars and drove away. Carolyn drove to Emily's home with Jed following her. She helped her boss out of the car and asked for her keys.

'Oh dear me,' Emily kept saying. 'Why?'

'It's just one of those awful things, Emily. A complete accident. Have you got the insurance details here at home? You can phone them and explain.'

'I have, but I don't feel they're going to take this seriously.'

'Whyever not? It was an accident. Horrible, but an accident.'

'Was it, though? I'm not so sure.'

'What on earth do you mean?'

'Oh . . . nothing. Forget it. Of course it was an accident. I'm talking through my hat. Now, I'm feeling much better than I was, so you can go off with that boyfriend of yours. Enjoy your trip to Cornwall.'

'You're absolutely sure you don't want me to stay and help you sort things out?'

'Course I'm sure. Go on. Enjoy.'

'Okay, I will. But promise me you'll take it easy. Don't come to any decisions in a hurry.'

'I'm fine now, thank you. It was really just the shock. And forget what I said about accidents or not. Of course it was an accident.'

Carolyn walked back to Jed's car thoughtfully. She was troubled by Emily's words. It sounded as though something was not quite as it seemed. She mentioned it to Jed as they drove to her flat. 'She kept asking herself if it really was an accident. What do you think she meant?'

'No idea. Perhaps she felt she shouldn't have left the computers turned on. They should have been fine, but you never know.'

'Maybe. We've never had a problem before. They've always been left on. Oh dear, I really don't like leaving at this point in time.'

'Stop it. We're going to go to Cornwall in the morning. Tonight, if you prefer. You could always go and pack right now and we can set off this afternoon. How about it?'

'I couldn't possibly. I have a stack of

ironing to do, and then I have to decide what I'm taking.'

'Bring it with you. I've got a perfectly good iron. Paul's busy tonight anyway, so I was only going to be sitting by myself.'

'But I've got sheets and other stuff to do.'

'Do them when you get back. You won't have to go to work. Come on, let's go and get you packed. I'll leave a note for Paul, and we can easily be in Cornwall by the evening.'

'You make it sound tempting.'

'Then be tempted. There's nothing to keep us here.'

She glanced at her watch. It was only just after ten o'clock. Could she possibly do everything and be ready to go?

'Okay,' she decided, 'drop me at home, then go and pack and come back and pick me up. Cornwall, here we come.'

'That's wonderful. I promise you won't be disappointed. I'll be back to collect you at eleven thirty.'

'That's much too soon.'

'Be ready, or I'll go on my own and leave you behind.' He pulled up outside her flat. 'You'll only need shorts and T-shirts. Something warmer for the evening. It can get chilly. Oh, and bring something for wet weather. It does rain just occasionally in Cornwall. I'll see you at eleven thirty.'

Carolyn ran up the stairs and let herself in. She felt slightly panicked and started dashing round, then stopped herself and took out the ironing board. Half an hour later, she had ironed most of the things she planned to pack and put them into her suitcase. Eleven fifteen. She stuffed the board away and left the rest of her ironing for when she got back. She could hardly think that far ahead. Fridge. She needed to check what was in there and turn it off. For the next quarter of an hour she worked very hard, putting perishables into a carrier bag. She was almost ready when Jed rang her doorbell.

'Nearly done,' she said as she let him in. 'Just need to check the windows are all shut.'

'I'll do that.'

'Thanks. I think that's about it. I'm done. Anything that's left will still be here when I get back. Have you told Paul your latest mad scheme?'

'I called him at work,' Jed replied. 'He didn't mind, and seemed fine. I've even left his keys in the kitchen.'

'Very good. My case is ready to put in the car. And there's a carrier bag with odd bits and pieces in. We can use them up, can't we?'

'Course. Anything to feed us over the next few days.'

'Just some fruit and a few bits of vegetable. I've been running it down this week ready to leave tomorrow.'

Jed went downstairs with her bag, and she looked round. She loved her flat. It had been carefully decorated to fit in with her lifestyle. Uncluttered and simple, it was a prime example of her work. For a moment she thought about

Henry and wondered where he was hiding. It had all been so strange, the way he had disappeared so suddenly. Why hadn't he even tried to contact her? She gave a sigh. Henry was part of her past now. She might never know what had happened to him. Perhaps he had found someone else and had cancelled the wedding for that reason. But Carolyn would never actually believe that. They had been much too close for her to fail to be aware of something like that.

'Oh Henry,' she muttered, 'I really hope you're all right.'

She went out and locked the door, then ran down to Jed and a week in Cornwall.

6

It took three and a half hours to reach Exeter. Carolyn had fallen asleep, and when Jed stopped the car she jolted awake. 'Where are we?' she asked.

'Exeter services,' Jed replied. 'I needed a break. Had a good sleep?'

'I suppose I must have done. How much further is it?'

'Couple of hours or thereabouts, maybe a bit less. Depends on the traffic. You want something to eat?'

'Yes, please.'

'Come on then, let's get out and we'll see what they've got. And we can do some shopping for supper. Thought you'd prefer to eat at home after the journey.'

'Sounds perfect.'

The café was very busy and it took them a while to get served. They bought sandwiches and coffee and sat outside with them, then went back inside and bought steak, some salad, and a loaf of bread from the little supermarket. Jed insisted on paying, as Carolyn was his guest.

'Keep your money,' he said. 'You might need it if you haven't got a job anymore.'

She frowned. 'You're right. I somehow doubt Emily will want to start up again. She's been ready to retire for quite a while now. I suppose I'll have to start looking for something else. With any luck, I shouldn't find it too hard. I'm still youngish, but I'm also experienced. It'll just be a case of finding a company with vacancy.'

'You could always start on your own.'

'Oh right, of course. Like heck I could.' She gave a rather wry smile. 'I'll wait and see what happens. Gosh, when I think of that burnt-out wreck of a place and compare it to what was once there . . . it's horrific.'

'You should try to stop thinking about it,' Jed said gently.

They left the services area and drove onto the A30. 'This is where I feel I'm getting closer,' Jed said. 'It seems sort of peaceful, don't you think?'

'I suppose so, yes. The mad traffic has calmed down at least.'

'Quite a long way to go yet. You can go back to sleep if you want to.'

'I don't even know where you live.'

'In a tiny village, in the far west. Only about half a dozen houses. I'm currently renting my place from a local farmer. I'd really like to buy it, but he's not willing to sell. It's quite an old cottage, actually. Not unlike Paul and Mel's place.'

'Sounds nice.'

'I love it there. This time of year is rather lovely in Cornwall. Lots of wild flowers around. The bird life is good too. Lots of baby birds learning to fly.'

'Sounds perfect for a photographer.'

They drove for the next hour and at last arrived at Tregorwen. It was almost seven o'clock, and both of them were starving. They unpacked the car and

Jed headed to the kitchen to start cooking.

'You can go and unpack if you like,' he suggested.

'Wouldn't you like some help with dinner?'

'From what you say about your cooking skills, I can probably manage better on my own. But thanks for the offer.'

'I'm pretty good at salad. And I can lay tables quite satisfactorily.'

He took her upstairs and showed her into a small but perfect bedroom. It was pretty but not fussy, and she loved the plain blue curtains against the matching striped wallpaper. There was a double bed taking up most of the space, and a small wardrobe and drawers to one side.

Jed laid her case on the bed. 'I'll have a glass of something ready for you when you come down,' he promised. 'Oh, the bathroom is over there. You can look at my room, too, if you're interested.' He had guessed exactly what she planned to do. She grinned and said she'd be down in a few minutes.

She peered through the tiny window. She could see a strip of bright blue in the distance that she took to be the sea. Immediately outside the window, she could see a pretty garden. There were loads of flowers spilling out of borders onto the small lawn. She must ask Jed how much was already there when he moved in, and how much he had done. Was it all his furniture, or the cottage owner's? *Interrogation time*, she laughed to herself.

Carolyn opened her case and took out her clothes, hanging them in the wardrobe. Suddenly, the aroma of cooking onions floated up the stairs, and her tummy rumbled. She stuffed the rest of her things into the drawers and rushed downstairs.

'Glass of red okay for you?' Jed asked.

'Wonderful, thank you. Can I do something to help?'

'Sit and talk to me.'

'Oh I can do that, all right. Talking for Britain is what I do best.'

'What do you think of the cottage?'

'It's lovely,' Carolyn said with a grin. 'Really nice. The farmer obviously has good taste.'

'What do you mean?'

'I assume he or his wife was responsible for the furniture and decoration?'

'Nope, that was all me. This place was pretty much a wreck when I found it. Everything you've seen represents many hours of hard labour. In return, I get it for a pittance in rent. Unfortunately, the owner now reckons it's worth a lot of money, so I just have to hope he doesn't sell it until I'm ready to leave. Problem is, I think I like it here and don't see myself ready to move any time soon.'

'Perhaps you should get a valuation from an estate agent or three. See what they think it may be worth, and then you can make him an offer.'

'Doubt if I could afford any sort of

offer he'd expect. When it was a wreck, it was quite different. I could have afforded it in those days.'

'How long did it take you?'

'About eighteen months altogether. I was camping here for a lot of the time. He paid for most of the basic stuff, and I bought the furniture and did the decorating. Glad you like it, anyway. Right, we're just about ready to eat. There's cutlery in the drawer beside you.'

Carolyn took out knives and forks and put them on the table, while Jed produced a bowl of salad from the fridge. Goodness knew when he'd made that, she thought. As she dug her knife into the steak, she gave him a huge grin.

'Looks delicious,' she said. 'Thank you so much.'

'My pleasure entirely. Tomorrow, I'll show you round the area. There are some lovely little coves near here. Almost secret sorts of places that few people know about.'

'Sounds lovely.'

It was a pleasant evening, and by ten o'clock they were both yawning, so they decided to have an early night. Carolyn fell asleep quickly, dreaming about what had seemed an endless journey in the car.

★   ★   ★

Unknown to either of them, Henry was living about five miles away. In another small hamlet, he'd rented a tiny cottage, and had even found himself a job working in a small shop. It was very different from anything he'd ever done before, and he was rather enjoying the lack of responsibility and being able to get up each morning without any worries. Well, that was perhaps a slight exaggeration. He was constantly looking over his shoulder, expecting to see someone from his old life chasing him. But he felt reasonably safe in his hidden corner of the country, and felt content.

He'd even got over the horrendous thing he'd done to the woman he'd believed he loved. Having given it much thought, Henry realised he couldn't possibly have loved Carolyn the way he thought, if he'd been able to do that to her. He wasn't even bothered by the fact that he'd left some of his possessions in their flat. It had always been Carolyn's flat, anyway. It was her inheritance that had bought it, and though he had helped with painting and simple stuff, it had always been her choice that won out in the end. Whatever he'd done to hurt her, Henry hoped she'd forgiven him and wasn't sitting at home alone brooding over him.

He put on his shirt with the slogan of the shop written on the pocket and set off for his day's work. The shop's owner had also let him the cottage, so it was a convenient arrangement all round. She was waiting for him to arrive and said she was going out for the day.

'My grandchildren need looking after, so I hope you don't mind taking care of things here for me,' she said.

'There's a delivery coming at some point, but I doubt you'll be so busy you can't see to it. Okay?'

'That's fine, thank you,' he replied. 'Shall I unpack it?'

'If you've got the time. Check it all, mind. Then you can put it in the stockroom.'

'Right you are, Demelza. Have a nice day, and don't worry about the shop. I can easily manage it.'

He did actually think life would be easier if she wasn't there fussing round most of the time. He got on with her quite well, but she was always chatting and asking him things about his past. And he'd invented quite a past for himself. Widowed about two years ago, he was now trying to rediscover himself, he'd told her, and this was proving a perfect opportunity. At times, he almost believed his story himself. It was a rather solitary life, but he felt he needed this time and space.

Then someone came into the shop, and he started his day.

* ★ ★

Back at Jed's home, they were waking to a lovely morning. Carolyn got up first and went downstairs and took a mug of coffee out into the garden. There were birds singing and she could hear the buzz of bees as they searched for nectar among the roses. The sun felt warm on her shoulders and she wondered if she ought to go and find her sunglasses. She stretched out lazily and felt very content. In some ways she felt she was over Henry, and that was undoubtedly due to this new man, Jed.

But how did she really feel about him? He was lovely, she thought, and in time, she might even find him most attractive — but it was too soon after Henry. What was her ex-fiancé doing? she wondered. His expertise in computers would surely mean he'd easily get another job. In fact, she had no real idea where on earth he was. He might even have gone abroad somewhere. Hong Kong or Singapore. She'd got over hating him for what he had done. He might even have done her a favour. It would have been terrible to have got married and then discovered they wanted to split up.

'I hope you're all right, Henry,' she muttered.

'Talking to yourself?' Jed asked as he came into the garden. 'I saw you'd boiled the kettle, so I've made some coffee for myself too. Lovely morning, isn't it?'

'Certainly is.'

'Did you sleep well?'

'Marvellously, thank you. How about you?'

'Yes, fine. What do you want to eat? I can offer you toast, or toast, or perhaps toast?'

'I think toast might be a good choice, thanks.'

'Good girl. Toast it is. I'll go and sort it.'

'I'll come and help.'

'No, you stay there. You make a nice picture against the garden flowers. I might even dig out my camera.'

'Don't you dare. I'm in no state to be photographed.'

'I don't agree. I like pictures of people being relaxed. You stay there; I won't be long.'

Carolyn sat where she was, feeling distinctly lazy. In a few minutes, Jed came out with a tray, which he set down on the small table. 'Come and get it. I've made some more coffee. Proper stuff this time, none of your instant. Toast and honey do for you?'

'Lovely. But you really don't need to wait on me, you know.'

'I'm happy to do it. But after today, you can take a share while I do some work. I need to take a few pictures for a company who want to promote their holiday letting business. You can come along if you're interested, or I can drop you somewhere to wander.'

'Sounds good. I'll tag along with you. Tomorrow, you say?' She was spreading delicious golden honey on her toast and then took a mouthful. 'Oh wow. I've died and gone to heaven. What sort of honey is this?'

'It's a local heather honey. I buy it at a little shop I know.'

'It's wonderful. I must take some back with me.'

'We'll call in sometime during the week.'

They chatted for a while, planning some things they were going to do, including a trip to the shops to buy supplies.

'Actually, I might need to do some shopping quite soon,' Jed said. 'Apart from the basics, there's very little to eat in the place. I've got a small freezer, but it's practically empty from before I went away.'

'Looks like it's the supermarket first. Then perhaps we can walk down to the sea? Doesn't look too far from here.'

'Okay. We'll do just that.'

'And please, let me buy some of the stuff,' Carolyn offered. 'If I'm going to be eating it, that seems fair to me.'

'You don't have a job anymore. You

need to save the pennies. You don't know when you'll be working again.'

Carolyn frowned. She'd forgotten the implications of the fire and felt almost sick when she thought about it. 'I wonder how Emily is?' she mused. 'Hope she's not feeling too down in the dumps. Maybe I should call her.'

'I'd leave her to get over it for the weekend.'

'Oh goodness, I'd quite forgotten it was Saturday. Do you really have to work tomorrow? It'll be Sunday.'

'Afraid so. Tomorrow is changeover day and the only time the properties will be vacant for an hour or two. I need to get inside and take some shots. If I go around lunchtime, they'll be cleaned and ready for the next lot to come in.'

'Quite complicated, isn't it?'

'They're quite good clients. They own a lot of properties around this part of the county. Often renew their brochures, so more pictures for me. Right. Eaten and drunk enough? Shall we go?'

'Shall I wash up?'

'Nah. We'll do it later. Come on, let's go and hit the local town. There's even a choice of supermarkets.'

They drove to Penzance and decided to have a walk in the town before shopping. The harbour looked delightful in the sunshine. Jed led Carolyn up to the top of the stairs in the shopping precinct and looked over the wall.

'Wow, that's such a good view,' she said. 'So many little boats in there. Oh, it's so beautiful.' She sniffed the sea air, loving it.

'You want to look in the shops in the town?'

'A little look, perhaps. But I do want to go to the sea.'

They walked through the arcade and into Market Jew Street. There were a number of empty shops. 'Oh dear, looks as if it's got the same disease as back home,' Carolyn commented. 'So many shops closing down, presumably because of the business rates.'

'Well, that and lack of decent

business. Not much fun being a shopkeeper these days, I guess.'

'I suppose not. Maybe I won't open a shop after all,' Carolyn said with a laugh.

'I'd wondered whether to open somewhere myself. Sell some of my pictures and maybe make some cards too. But it simply isn't worth it. If I did, I'd need someone to manage the shop while I was out taking pictures. You don't fancy doing that, do you?' Jed said jokingly.

'Pay me enough and I might. Come on, let's leave this lot and go and paddle. Well, maybe we should go shopping first if we want to eat again.'

It was an interesting experience for Carolyn. Seeing how different people did their shopping fascinated her. She often pottered round quite slowly, looking at the different things and making her decision. With Jed, it was wham-bam. He walked along each aisle and picked up what he wanted with no thought for looking at different choices.

'You like ice-cream?' he asked.

'Oh yes, love it.'

'Good. What sort?'

'Don't mind.'

'Right, I'll get this one then. It'll do as a sweet. I'm not really into sweets.'

'Nor me. But ice-cream sounds wonderful.'

'Good. Anything else you'd like?'

'I think you've got everything.'

'I just need some fruit. Can't have you fainting away for lack of vitamins.' Jed chuckled. 'Right, let's get this show on the road.'

They soon were home again and unpacked the shopping. Once everything was put away, Jed looked at the time. 'Heavens. It's almost half past two. You must be starving.'

'I am rather hungry,' Carolyn admitted.

'We'll go down to the beach and pick up some grub. Nothing like sitting on a Cornish beach eating pasties.'

They set off to walk down to the beach. There was a little shop on the way, where they bought pasties. 'Oh gosh, they smell wonderful,' Carolyn enthused. 'Can't we eat them as we walk along?'

'Be my guest.' They munched them, holding them in the paper bags.

'My first genuine Cornish pasty,' Carolyn said as she screwed up the bag. 'They really do taste different here. Must be the Cornish air.'

'Guess so. And we're not even on the beach yet.'

The cove was very small and quiet, and there was only one other family on the beach. Carolyn was speechless until Jed asked what she thought of it.

'It's so beautiful. I can really see why you are so in love with the place.'

'Loving is easy with somewhere like this,' he said enigmatically. He knew he was beginning to fall in love with this woman, but he didn't want to say anything — not just yet. He knew about her loss and didn't want to frighten her off. He really hoped they might have a future together. The timing was perfect.

She hadn't got a job and she was here, in his place, in his own surroundings. *Caution, Jed,* he told himself severely. *Don't let yourself say anything that will ruin things.*

7

Jed was up early the next morning. Carolyn heard him singing — rather tunelessly, she had to admit, but he did sound happy. He was sorting out his cameras ready for his job later. She heard him put the kettle on, and stretched lazily. She really ought to get up, but she felt warm and cosy here in her bed. The sun was shining behind the curtains, giving a blue haze to her room. She heard Jed coming upstairs, and he tapped at her door.

'Come in,' she called. 'I'm still in bed.'

'I've brought you some breakfast,' he said, manoeuvring his way through her door.

'Oh my goodness,' she said sitting up in surprise. 'I thought it was just a cup of coffee or tea.'

'I need to get moving before too

long. It'll take me a while to drive over to the village and I don't want to be late. You don't have to come if you'd prefer to stay here.'

'No, I want to come. I was just being lazy.'

'Right. Well enjoy breakfast, and I'll see you downstairs in a bit.'

'Thanks very much.' She buttered the toast and enjoyed more of the delicious local honey, washed down with excellent coffee. She felt rather luxurious, lying there. It was most unusual for her to feel spoilt like this. She certainly couldn't remember Henry ever doing anything like this for her. If they ever had breakfast in bed, it was down to her to prepare it.

She thought about Jed. He was certainly a catch for someone. He was good-looking, seemed relaxed, and was certainly very nice. She thought about his fiancée, or rather ex-fiancée, and realised she was actually quite glad the woman had gone off and left him. Even if it was too soon for Carolyn to consider him as a romantic interest, she felt pleased that she could.

She finished her toast and moved the tray to one side. It was time to get moving.

They drove along the main road for a while, and then Jed turned off into what looked like little more than a narrow cart track. There was even grass growing along its middle. 'I hope you know where we're going,' Carolyn commented.

'I think it's down here. I haven't been here before, but this sounds like the place she described when she phoned me. We should see some buildings quite soon.'

They drove on some way, and then suddenly they found themselves in a wide courtyard with several buildings round the edge. 'This looks a bit of all right, don't you think?'

'It looks gorgeous. A real haven.'

'Well that's exactly what it's called. Haven Holiday Homes.'

'Very appropriate,' Carolyn said with

a smile. 'Looks as if the cleaners are still working in some of the places.'

'I expect they'll be here for quite a while. I'll work round them. Now, are you ready to be my assistant?'

'Don't ask me to photograph anything,' she squeaked in alarm. 'Put me behind a camera and I cut off everyone's vital parts.'

'I was thinking you could help me to carry stuff in. Look after the tripods and so on.'

'Think I might manage that. I'll even try not to drop anything.'

'Good start. Okay, I'll go and see the boss first and see where she wants us to be. Come on, I'll introduce you as my chief assistant.'

Carolyn rather liked feeling a part if it all and got out of the car, following Jed across the courtyard. He knocked at the door of the largest house, which was soon answered.

'Yes? Oh, Mr Soames.'

'Jed, please. This is my assistant, Carolyn. Carolyn, meet Mrs Jacobs.'

'How do you do,' Carolyn said, wondering what else to say. 'What a lovely place you have here.'

'Thank you. We've done it all ourselves. It was once a series of old barns, and I saw the potential in converting them. We found some good builders locally, and here we are. But do come inside. I'm sorry, I always get carried away when someone comes for the first time.'

They followed her in through a delightful hall with a flagstone floor and several brightly coloured rugs. 'Come into the lounge. Or if you don't mind, come into the kitchen and I'll make some coffee.'

'Thanks very much,' Jed said. 'I just need to know exactly how you want me to take the pictures.'

The kitchen was every woman's dream: oak fittings all round, with every convenience one could think of. Mrs Jacobs went over to one of the sinks and pushed cups under a tap. 'Hope you don't mind instant. This tap is so much quicker than the machine,' she remarked, filling the mugs with boiling water.

'Wow, that's terrific. Boiling water on tap.' Carolyn was impressed.

'Saves a lot of time. Now, sugar and milk are there. Help yourselves.'

Carolyn sat quietly, listening to them discussing the new website Jed was to create and the brochure Mrs Jacobs wanted. Carolyn was surprised by Jed's professionalism, but then it was his business.

'So, if you'd like to send me your text, I'll incorporate it and send you the proofs back,' he said. 'Once approved, we can go live.'

'So how long might this take?'

Jed looked at Carolyn. 'I could start work on it right away, and we could be live in . . . well, as short a time as you like. Couple of days?'

'That's amazing. It'll probably take me a day or two to put words together.'

They went on to discuss the various units on the site and what was required in the way of pictures. There were four separate buildings and each one was quite different. Carolyn was beginning to get quite excited by the thought of looking at them. Mrs Jacobs picked up several bunches of keys and showed them round. The cleaners were all working, so it was a case of looking first and then deciding where to take pictures.

'Right, I think I have the gist of what you need,' Jed said after the tour. 'We'll take several pictures of the interiors, to show the rooms. I'll take some pictures of the whole courtyard as well, and perhaps we can incorporate a click device to pick out individual properties. Then you can click on it to enter each one separately. Yes, I'll try that and send it to you for your approval. What I need from you is a general introduction and a sheet of costs. I can put this in as appropriate. Good. I'll get my cameras.'

'I'm so glad I remembered you. You're exactly what I needed. I can't wait.' Mrs Jacobs obviously liked everything Jed had said and was ready to go with whatever he suggested. 'My husband will be delighted that he doesn't have to deal with it. Take whatever pictures you need. I'm sure you'll manage to avoid the cleaners. I'd like some of each property — bedrooms, living room, and kitchen. I'll leave it to you.'

'No worries. I'll sort it all out and let you see what I've taken afterwards.'

Jed went to the car, followed by Carolyn, and he picked up several bags with cameras and lights and asked her to carry some of them. He set about making his pictures count and took several of each setting. Carolyn was amazed at the amount of time it took, and watched in fascination. She had no idea what she might have called snaps of each room could need so much perfection. He muttered all the way through and she asked him to repeat himself a few times, until she realised he was muttering to himself. It was almost three o'clock before he pronounced himself satisfied.

'Good. That'll do me nicely,' he told her. 'Come on, let's say goodbye and get on our way. Sorry it took so long. You must be starving.'

'I am pretty peckish,' Carolyn admitted.

They went to the main house to say goodbye. 'Come in,' said Mrs Jacobs. 'I've put a few snacks together for you. You must be feeling hungry by now. Nothing special, of course.'

'That's very good of you,' Carolyn said as they followed her into the kitchen. 'Nothing special? Looks like a proper feast to me.' There was pâté, ham, salad, and a delicious-looking crusty loaf of bread.

'This is terrific — thank you very much,' Jed echoed her feelings.

Soon they were all sitting with full plates and enjoying the unexpected treat. Mrs Jacobs ate with them, commenting that she hadn't expected them to take quite so long.

'I had to make sure the lighting was right and get proper angles,' Jed explained. 'It makes all the difference to the results if you get it all right. I hope you'll like what I've done.'

'I'm sure it'll be perfect. Are you sure the price you quoted will cover your work?'

'Of course. Besides, you're feeding us rather well, too.'

'But your web design — that will take you extra time, won't it? I'd be happy to pay you for it.'

'I'll see how long it takes. But don't worry about it. I won't charge much more anyway.'

When they had all eaten as much as they wanted, Jed and Carolyn thanked Mrs Jacobs and left the lovely property.

'Who would know all that is hidden down that little lane?' Carolyn remarked. 'You ought to have taken a picture of the entrance, otherwise people will find it tricky to spot.'

'Blimey, why didn't I think of that? Do you mind if we go back? Won't take long. Just a quick stop and snap.'

Jed turned the car round and went back to the entrance to the property. He parked a little way along the road, picked up a camera, and ran back. He seemed to have taken several shots, Carolyn thought. Good job it was all digital and he didn't have to fiddle about with prints too.

When they were home again, Jed seemed rather distracted as he asked her what she wanted to do.

'I suspect you want to download your pictures and take a look at what you've got,' she replied. 'Am I right?'

He looked rather shamefaced. 'Well, yes. I am keen to make sure the pictures are all good.'

'Then do it. I'm fine. Might go for a walk, or just sit out in the garden.'

'If you're sure. I'll organise something for supper later on.'

'Don't worry about it. Go on, enjoy yourself. Look at your pictures.'

Without further ado, he turned on his computer and started to download his morning's work. Carolyn listened to his grunts and then his appreciative sounds. She shook her head and went outside. It was a lovely early evening, and she sat quietly listening to the birds and enjoying the peace.

She dozed off and awoke some time later, feeling chilly. When she went inside, she saw that Jed was working with deep concentration. She looked over his shoulder and was very impressed.

'Oh, hi. What time is it?' he asked.

'Nearly seven.'

'Oh dear. I'd better stop doing this and find something for supper.'

'If you don't mind me rummaging in your freezer, I'll do something.'

'Don't mind at all. But are you sure you can manage? I'd rather come and do it myself than clear up some burnt remains.'

'Cheek. I can do simple things. I'll see what I can find.'

'There may be some fish in there. You can't go far wrong with that.' He went back to his work on the computer.

An hour later Carolyn came back into the room, saying supper was ready when he was. He came into the kitchen and she proudly drew her fish pie out of the oven. 'Wow,' he commented. 'That looks wonderful.'

'See? I can cook some things. Okay, I admit I cheated a bit. Used a can of soup instead of making sauce, but I hope you like it.'

'I'm sure I'll love it. Makes a change for someone else to cook for me. I appreciate it.'

When they had cleared the dishes, Jed invited Carolyn to come and look at the work he'd been doing. She sat at his computer and clicked through the pictures, and finally said, 'Wow. They really are very good. You've made everywhere look so appealing.'

'Click on one of the doors and see what happens,' he invited. She did, and was immediately taken into each of the properties in turn. 'That's terrific. You're very clever. At least as good as

Henry . . . Sorry, I should never have said that.'

'It's okay. I'll take it as a compliment. I'm sure you meant it that way.'

'It was his job. He made his living by working on computers, so of course he was good. But it's not fair of me to compare the two of you.'

'I used to make my living on computers too. I try to keep up, but they change so quickly, and I barely do. But I know how to manipulate things to get the results I want.'

'I didn't realise. What made you give that up, then?'

'My ex worked in the same company. I sort of went off in a flurry of bad temper when she left, and decided to change everything.'

'What a shame,' Carolyn sympathised.

'Yes and no. It meant that I followed my dream and took up photography in earnest. And I'm happy now. I don't have anyone else to worry about. At least . . . '

'At least what?'

'Oh, nothing. So you like what I've done so far with the pictures?'

'I think they're terrific. Mrs J will be certain to like them.'

'Thanks. I hope so.' Jed sat back and sighed. 'I don't think there's much more I can do now, so let's relax. Anything on TV?'

'The usual Sunday night stuff.'

'Let's slump, then. I do feel weary after all our efforts today. We can sit and watch something and decide what we're doing tomorrow.'

'Suits me fine. I do feel a bit sleepy. Must be the Cornish air. I haven't done anything, really.'

'Lots of folk say the air here is tiring. Maybe it's just that you've stopped working so hard.'

'Gosh, yes. I wonder what sort of weekend Emily's had. Not good, I bet.'

'Maybe not. But there's nothing you can do about it. Come on, relax and enjoy it.'

* ★ ★

The next few days went by in a whirl. They visited lots of local places and some more distant ones. Wherever he went, Jed carried his camera. He took lots of pictures, which Carolyn thought were excellent, but he pooh-poohed them and deleted them. She was amazed he could do that so frequently, but he complained something wasn't quite right or he'd got the wrong angle.

'I'd be delighted to have done anything so good,' she told him.

'I'll show you some of the ones I'm really pleased with. Then you'll see the difference.'

She realised she was beginning to feel something for this really rather gorgeous man. He'd not so much as tried to kiss her, for which she felt truly grateful. She still felt it was early days since her breakup from Henry, and Jed obviously respected her feelings.

That evening, Jed took out a large file. 'Here are some of my favourite pictures. Look at them and you'll see why I deleted so many of the ones I took recently. These are so much better.' He passed a series of large photos to her, one by one.

'Oh my goodness. These are wonderful.' She looked through them all and was lost for words. 'You really are very good. I thought your pictures of the buildings we visited were excellent, but these are quite outstanding. You could win prizes for some of them.' He seemed to blush and looked away. 'You *have* won prizes, haven't you?'

'I have, yes.'

'What did you win?'

'Oh, nothing much. Well, I did win quite a substantial cheque, actually. A major competition. But it's living in such a beautiful place that does it. It's the scenery, not me.'

'Which one won?'

'I've only got a small copy. It was a sunset. Hang on, I'll find it in a minute.' He foraged through another folder and produced the most glorious picture of a sunset. It was a deep magenta tinged with oranges, a cerulean blue tipping the picture at the bottom.

'Goodness. How did you manage to capture that one? The sea looks amazing over the bottom of it. Where was it?'

'Just outside here. It was taken in early spring at the end of a perfect day. If there had been any clouds they would have been a pinky-orange colour. But there weren't on this occasion. Hence I could capture the whole scene in its perfection. I have to admit, I was very pleased. Raised my profile somewhat.'

'I should think so. I have to say, I'm impressed. You have a real talent for composition. How on earth do you get everything into the picture?'

'It's the way I look at things,' he said with a smile. 'Anyway, there are loads more if you really want to see them.'

'Yes please. I've always loved seeing people's holiday pictures, but these are in quite a different category. People would want to hang them on their walls.'

'I've had some canvas prints made, which are hanging in various places around. I make a bit out of each one. Keeps me going, that and special commissions — like the brochure and website I did for Mrs Jacobs. Which reminds me, I still haven't had her approval for the stuff I sent in. Excuse me a minute. I'll email her and ask her if she's received it all.'

Carolyn sat looking through more of his pictures. She loved the ones of trees and grass. The close-ups of leaves and flowers were equally inspiring.

At last, Jed came back to sit beside her, saying Mrs Jacobs had loved all he'd done and was more than ready for him to take the stuff to the printer's. 'We'll go tomorrow if that's okay,' he said. 'I'll show you some of the delights of Truro. It's a nice town; quite busy, with lots of small independently owned shops. There are the large retail chains there too, of course, but it's the smaller places that give it character.'

'I'll look forward to it. I don't know about you, but I wouldn't mind an early night.'

'If that's what you want to do. I might stay up a while longer and do some stuff on the computer. If you don't mind, that is.'

'Course not. It's your home. I mustn't forget to visit your little shop and get some honey before I go. Can't believe how quickly the week's gone.'

'It's simply sped by. It's been great having you here. Can't you stay on a while longer?'

'I've almost run out of clean clothes,' she giggled. 'Can't go round with dirty underpants, now, can I?'

'If that's the only reason, use the washer. Please stay on for a while longer, Carolyn. You haven't got to get back for work, after all.'

'Let me think about it. I'm going up to bed now, but I promise I'll think about it.'

'I'll let you off with that. Good night,

love.' He rose, and as she got up he leaned forward to kiss her. It was brief but firm, and Carolyn had no time to assess her feelings before it was over.

'Sorry. I didn't mean to do that,' he said.

'It's all right,' she whispered. 'But I'm still going up to bed.'

8

Carolyn lay in bed and found she was shivering. It was ridiculous; she wasn't cold at all. It must be because Jed had kissed her. She had to admit, she had rather liked it. She really must stop feeling so guilty. After all, Henry probably wasn't feeling guilty in any way. Jed, she knew, was footloose and fancy-free. And maybe he, too, was falling for her. Her shivering increased and she sat up. This was quite silly. She grabbed her dressing gown and went downstairs again. Jed looked up.

'What's up?' he asked.

'I don't know. I think you've had some sort of effect on me.'

'I did say I was sorry,' he told her. 'You just looked so lovely, and we'd had such a nice time together.'

'Whatever it was, it's stopped me from sleeping. Maybe I'm starting to get over what Henry did to me.'

'That's good. I knew some concentrated Jed would be good for you. My own brand of special therapy. Works wonders, you know.'

'I wanted to say, well, thank you. Thank you for being so patient with me. I can't be the easiest person to put up with.'

'Nonsense. You've been great to have around. I'm desperately trying to control myself,' he added.

'Really? You do surprise me. Does this mean . . . well, that you like me?'

'Like you? Of course I *like* you. Just so you know, I'm prepared to wait as long as you need till you're ready to think about having someone else in your life.' He paused and looked at her carefully, as if trying to assess the effect his words were having on her. She smiled at him and he immediately felt more confident. 'I know it's still too soon for you to make any sort of commitment, but I want you to know I'm here for you. Waiting for the right time.'

'Oh Jed, you're very kind. I'm sorry to be such a wimp, but I'm still a bit . . . wobbly.'

'I know, love. As I say, I'm here for you.'

'Thank you.' She leaned over and kissed him, very gently. 'I'll remember what you said, and I promise I won't leave you hanging on for too long. And yes, please, I would like to stay on a while longer. Assuming you do indeed have a working washing machine.'

'That's terrific. Do you want to put your washing in now? I can get it ready for you.' He leapt off his seat and went towards the kitchen.

Carolyn laughed. 'Tomorrow will be fine. I've still got one pair of clean knickers!'

She ran upstairs and settled down, then fell asleep quickly, smiling to herself. Jed came up some time later and, with a sigh, went to his own room. He lay awake for ages, thinking about his future and whether it would actually include this woman who had made such an impact on him. Perhaps it was almost time to try a different tactic.

* * *

The next morning, Carolyn came down with a large bundle of washing. She had included her wet towels, hoping they'd be dry enough to use again once they were washed. She stuffed it all into the machine and stared at the control panel. It was a more modern machine than she was used to and she scratched her head, wondering what to do next. She decided to wait till Jed got here and let him sort it out.

Wandering into the kitchen, she switched on the kettle and made some coffee. Then she opened the back door, planning to take it outside, but just then it started to rain. She cursed. Her washing was going to stay wet if she couldn't hang it out. Still, it was the first rain they'd had all week, so she couldn't really complain. She went back into the lounge and put the television on. It was almost nine by the time her host arrived.

'Sorry,' he said. 'Didn't sleep all that well. Must have drifted off in the small hours and then slept through. How are you?'

'I'm fine, thanks. I've put my washing in the machine but wasn't sure which programme to use or where you put the soap powder.'

'I'll see to it. More coffee?'

'I can come and do it,' she protested. 'I don't expect you to do everything for me.'

'Don't worry about it. Stay where you are and I'll do it.'

'I'll come and sort out some breakfast. I wasn't really watching the TV. It was just on.'

'Anything new happening in the big wide world?'

'All the usual stuff.' She followed him into the kitchen and sorted their breakfast. 'We're nearly out of honey. Shall we go and get some more? It's raining, so maybe some shopping might be good.'

'I'll take you to my little shop,' Jed offered. 'It's only a small place and a bit off the beaten track. They specialise in local products.'

'Do they do pasties? I think it's about time we had more of them.'

He laughed. 'Got you hooked on the local food, have we? Yes, they do pasties.'

'Great. And no arguing — I'm paying today.'

'Okay, fine. I've always wanted to be a kept man. You can buy two pasties.'

'Not sure what I'll do with heaps of wet washing in this weather.'

'Not a problem. I have a tumble dryer. I was never prepared to festoon the place with wet washing. It's out in the garage.'

They set off for the little shop and were soon there, looking at a bewildering variety of local produce.

'The honey's over here,' Jed said, but Carolyn was standing transfixed, staring at the man who was sitting by the till. He was equally transfixed as he looked at her.

'Henry?' she muttered.

'Carolyn? What on earth are you doing here?'

'What on earth are *you* doing here?'

'I work here.'

'For how long? And why? Why aren't you working with computers?'

'I like it here.'

She felt weak at the knees and wondered how long she might remain standing. Her head buzzed and she thought she was about to faint. Jed came up to her and took her arm. She looked round at him, grateful for his intervention.

'I take it you two know each other?' he asked.

'This is Henry. My ... well, I suppose he's my ex.'

'How do you do? I'm Jed,' he said to the bemused Henry. 'Look, shall I leave you two alone for a while? You clearly have a lot to talk about.' He swung round and went out of the shop. The two looked at each other, their feelings in turmoil.

'I came . . . '

'How come . . . ' They both started to speak at the same time.

'Sorry, you go on,' said Carolyn.

'I drove down here after the . . . after we didn't get married. I'm so sorry. But I had to get as far away as possible. For your sake. I didn't want you to be harmed.'

'I don't understand what you're talking about. How could you? How on earth could you do it to me? To all our guests?'

'I'm sorry. It was the only thing I *could* do. You really don't know the whole story. It's possibly better if you don't. They might still come after you.'

'Who might? You're not making any sense. You need to tell me why you left me standing in my wedding dress, ready to commit to you forever.'

'I can't. Believe me, I never wanted to hurt you.'

'Huh,' she snorted. 'Well, you failed. I

was desperately hurt. I'll never forgive you, ever.'

'I deserve that.'

She looked away from him and tried very hard to work out what to do next. The breathing space she needed was granted to her by another customer coming into the shop.

'Morning,' the woman said. 'I want some biscuits. Got a friend coming round for tea and need some nice ones.' She went round the side of the shop and picked up what she wanted. 'Disappointing weather today, isn't it?' she said to Carolyn, who nodded and watched as the woman took her purchase to the till. 'Thanks a lot,' she said as she left.

'I'd never have seen you as a shop worker,' Carolyn said to Henry at last.

'I've quite enjoyed the change. No real worries and responsibilities. And there's nobody to try and get you to do things.' He stopped at that point.

'When did anyone ever try to make you do something?'

'I don't want to talk about it.'

'Oh, now, come on. The whole wedding thing, it was your idea. Remember? Let's get married, you said. Let's make it soon. You said you wanted to marry me. It was all down to you.' Her emotions started to rise to the surface, threatening to take her over. He must give her some answers.

'I'm sorry. But like I said, you don't know the whole story. I still can't tell you everything.'

'You're making no sense at all.' She looked into his eyes, as if trying to read his soul. How could someone who had declared his undying love for her have done what he did?

'Can we start again?' Henry asked her. 'If you moved down here, perhaps we could begin our lives over.'

'Oh no. Not for anything would I ever commit to you again. In fact, I think you did me a favour. If we had got married, I'd probably have got sick of you quite soon. When I think about it, I can see we weren't really suited; and it would have been a whole lot more complicated to separate after we'd married.'

Henry flinched. 'I deserve that, too. I can see you've moved on. This . . . what's-his-name — Jed? Well, good luck to you.'

'Jed is a very good friend. He's been marvellous to me. Very kind and understanding. But there's nothing else going on. And I still don't know why you ran away.'

'Look, it's about time I put the kettle on. Do you want some coffee?'

'I'd better not. Jed's waiting for me.'

Henry looked upset. He felt irrationally jealous of the man. 'Mustn't upset Jed, of course not.'

Carolyn felt he sounded bitter, but in the end, it was all his own doing. He had dumped her and she had moved on. 'We came in to get some honey. Perhaps I'd better get it and go.'

'Where are you staying?'

'With Jed. He's got a cottage near here.'

'I've met him before. He's been in the shop to buy honey a few times. Look, would you like to go out for a drink one night?'

'I don't think so. Besides, I'm supposed to be going home soon. And I don't have a car. Mine got stolen and torched.'

'What?' Henry went pale. 'From outside the flat?'

'I was at Paul's place. It was taken from there.'

'I suppose it is a bit of a rough area,' he said uncertainly.

'Not at all. Anyway, it means I don't have transport, so it would be rather awkward to try and meet up. And besides, I'm not sure I even want to see you again. You can't give me a reason for your actions, so I think it's time to say goodbye.'

Henry suddenly realised he was desperately lonely. He'd been almost happily moving along his track, not allowing himself any opportunity to meet people apart from in the shop, feeling gradually safer, sure that he was off the hook with the boss. For heaven's sake, he was still a young man with a future ahead of him. But seeing Carolyn had jolted him. Her car . . . Henry had a horrible feeling that maybe he wasn't as safe as he'd thought. And maybe his desertion hadn't made Carolyn any safer, either. But he was no longer working at Phoenix, so the criminals' demands couldn't be met. What else was he supposed to do?

He stared at the woman he had loved. If leaving her hadn't made any difference to her safety, and if they were both here, far from their old lives, surely their love could be rekindled?

'Please, Carolyn,' he began, 'please try and remember all the good times we had. Let's have a drink and see if we can't patch things up.'

'I'm sorry, Henry. I think in the interests of self-preservation, I have to say no.'

He could have laughed — she had no

idea how close to the mark she was.

Carolyn now felt more in control of herself and able to speak without feeling she was going to cry. 'I'll buy a couple of jars of honey and go. I wish you well and hope you'll be happy. Where's the honey?'

'Over there,' he said, pointing at the row of jars. 'Make your choice.'

She looked at the different types and felt confused. One of them she thought she recognised, so she picked up two jars of it. She paid for them and hurried out of the shop. Jed's car was empty, though. The rain had stopped and he'd obviously gone for a walk. She looked round, wondering which way he might have gone. She left the honey in the unlocked car and started to walk towards the sea. Her mind was whirling round.

She had almost reached the beach when she saw Jed walking back towards her. She looked hard at him. So different to Henry. He was considerably taller for a start, and his hair was as dark as Henry's was blond. But more importantly, he looked kinder. Less self-assured, in some ways. She stopped herself. It was odious to compare the two men, but she couldn't help it. She felt Jed was so open and honest, while Henry left much to be desired. He still had told her nothing about his reasons for calling off their wedding.

'Hi,' Jed called to her. 'Have you finished?'

'Oh yes. Quite finished.'

'Did he explain himself?'

'Not at all. He made one or two cryptic remarks about me getting harmed. I ask you! I told him he seemed quite capable of doing that to me himself.'

Jed took her hand and together they walked back to the car. Carolyn pulled her hand away before they reached the car, in case Henry might be watching. No need to rub it in. He clearly wasn't seeing another woman, or he'd never have asked her to go out for a drink with him. Everything involving him remained a mystery.

'I put the honey in the car,' she said. 'I saw it wasn't locked.'

'Oh, you got some?'

'I'm not sure it was exactly the same as the stuff you got, but I'm sure it can be changed if necessary.'

He glanced at it. 'No, it isn't the same. Shall I go and change it?'

'If you don't mind. I would, but I feel I've had my fill of Henry for one day.'

Jed picked up the two jars and went into the shop. He went straight to the counter and asked if he could exchange them.

'Sorry,' said Henry. 'Once it's been bought and paid for . . . The till, you know.'

'Oh for goodness' sake. It's the same price. Surely you can change it?'

'The bar code is recorded. Sorry, mate.'

'I'm not your mate. Never will be. Not after what you did to Carolyn. You really are a bastard, aren't you?'

'You know nothing about it. I was

only trying to protect her.'

'Seems like you're the only one she needs protecting from. Have you any idea how much you hurt her? She's well shot of you, that's all I can say.' Jed put the two jars back on the shelf and helped himself to two new jars. 'Thanks for your co-operation.' He swept out of the shop and left Henry standing by the counter looking totally gobsmacked.

'Any problems?' Carolyn asked as he returned to the car.

'None at all. He was sweetness personified.'

'Really?' she said.

'Really,' he repeated.

9

Carolyn was quiet as they drove home. Jed decided to leave her with her thoughts. He'd intended to go to Truro today, but somehow the events of the morning had put paid to his plans. He remembered they'd also planned to have pasties for lunch, and his mind ran through what was in the fridge. Nothing. Zero. Zilch. He spoke at last. 'We forgot to buy pasties,' he said.

'Oh yes. I'm afraid they were far from my mind.'

'I also need to go to Truro today. You don't have to come, if you'd prefer to stay at home. I'll do some shopping there too.'

'No, it's all right, I'll come. No point me sitting at home stewing, is there? Do you want to go straight there now?'

'I have to collect the stuff from home. And your washing will be finished by now too. I'm not sure what to offer you to eat. I think we're pretty well out of most things.'

They decided to go to Truro and buy pasties there. It would be a bit late for lunch, but it would fill the gap. They stopped in the cottage and took out the wash and put it into the tumble drier. Then Jed collected all the stuff for the printer and put it into a folder.

'Right. I'm ready, if you are.' Carolyn nodded and they set off. She was still rather quiet, and at last Jed asked her if she wanted to talk.

'I think I'm still confused. I mean, how can he possibly sit in that little shop all day and serve customers? He was always such a whizz kid with computers. He could make them do things that made my mind boggle. Now he's given it all up and is sitting in a shop.'

'Nothing wrong with being a shop-keeper. Perhaps he likes not having the pressure of a job where he's kept working all the time. I told you, I was working for a company like that. Then I came down here and took up my favourite hobby. Luckily for me, it's worked out and brings me a reasonable income. Enough for my simple life, anyway, and some left over for anyone to share it with me.' He looked hard at her, wondering what she would make of his remark. She didn't register anything.

They reached Truro and found a parking space in one of the multi-storey car parks.

'That was easy,' Carolyn said. 'I was expecting to be driving round for hours looking for somewhere to stop.'

'It's a bit late for the early shoppers so we're in luck. I'll call in at the printer's and then we'll find some pasties. There's a shop that sells lovely ones near the Pannier Market.'

She followed him through the cobbled streets and looked at some of the shops as they passed them. Somehow, shopping didn't really appeal to her. She had a whole lot of new clothes bought for the honey-moon that never was, and she couldn't face even looking at them. No, she was happiest in her collection of shirts and jeans. She didn't even have a job anymore, so her working clothes were now also redundant. Still, she would have to look for another job, so perhaps then they'd come back into use.

They reached the printer's and Jed leapt into action, describing exactly how he wanted the brochures printed, and then started negotiating the price. Carolyn smiled at his professional ease. He knew exactly how difficult the job was and how much time they'd need to spend on it. They reached a deal and he shook hands with the printer.

'I'll come and collect them on Monday, shall I?'

'Best give us till Tuesday, in case of any errors that may crop up.'

'All right, Tuesday it is. Is that OK with you, Carolyn?'

'Of course. Why wouldn't it be?'

'I was thinking about you needing to go back.'

'I hadn't thought that far ahead. If you're willing to put up with me, that's fine. Go for it.'

'Okay. I'll see you on Tuesday. Call me if there's any change.'

They left the print shop and walked back the way they'd come. 'Pasties next,' said Jed. Assuming you still want one?'

'Oh yes. Can we sit out on the big square to eat them?'

'The Piazza, you mean?'

'Whatever it's called. We can watch people go by. I love people-watching, don't you?'

'Of course. Only trouble is, I want to photograph them as they go by. Not all that many people allow that sort of behaviour.'

'Maybe they have guilty consciences. Don't want to be seen here or with someone they want kept secret.'

'You have a good imagination. I suspect it's more likely they feel scruffy

157

and not ready to be photographed. It's over here, the pasty shop.'

Soon they were sitting eating, along with several other people. It really was great-tasting food, Carolyn thought. No wonder pasties were popular all over the world.

'That was scrumptious,' she said as she ate the last bit of her pasty.

'You've got bits of pastry on your top. Here, let me brush them off.' Jed leaned over and brushed them away. 'You all right?'

'I think so. Yes, of course I am. Why wouldn't I be? In Truro with a good-looking, talented man, and I've just eaten a pasty.'

'That's okay then. Good-looking?' he queried, looking round. 'You must introduce me sometime. I'm sitting with a very beautiful young lady who could have any man she wanted.'

'Oh yes? Didn't do very well so far, did I?'

'Depends on what you want out of life.'

'Well, thank you for the compliment, anyway. So, what's next? Supermarket?'

He nodded and got up from his seat. It didn't take long to get to the supermarket and collect all they needed, and they were soon on their way back home.

'I wouldn't mind a walk down to the beach after we've unpacked,' Carolyn suggested when they'd almost arrived. 'I don't mind going on my own if you like.'

'Sounds like a good idea. I'd like to come with you, unless you need to be alone to digest this morning's encounter some more.'

She shook her head. 'I actually feel very calm about seeing Henry again. I really think I've moved on, even though it's less than two months since the wedding that never was. I think a lot of that is down to you, actually.'

'I'm very glad. You . . . must realise you've come to mean a lot to me?'

'I suspected. But it's still much too soon for me to be involved with anyone again. I'm sorry; I must be damaged goods. Second-hand rose, that's me.' She looked through the car window as she was speaking, hoping to hide from him the tears that were pricking at the back of her eyes.

'Here we are, home again. You okay now?'

'Yes, I'm fine. I'll grab these bags, shall I?'

They walked up the path and Jed unlocked the cottage door. He picked up a pile of letters from the mat. They both went into the kitchen and began to put away the shopping. He put the kettle on to make some tea, and Carolyn's mobile phone rang. She looked at the number, but it wasn't a familiar one.

'Hello?' she said hesitantly.

'Carolyn. It's me, Henry.'

'Henry, why are you calling me? And where are you calling from?'

Jed looked up when she said Henry's name and tactfully left her to it, taking his letters into the garden with him.

'I had to speak to you,' Henry said. 'After I saw you today, well, I realised everything I've lost.'

'It was your choice,' she snapped.

'Not really. I was forced into a corner I couldn't get out of. Look, can we meet? I really need to explain things to you properly. Perhaps then we . . . perhaps we could . . . '

'I don't think it's a good idea. I'm sorry, but no. I really can't.'

'Is that anything to do with the chap you were with?'

'No!'

'You're sleeping with him, I suppose?'

'Henry, it's none of your business who I sleep with. And I told you, Jed is a very good friend who is helping me out.'

'How long do you intend to stay in Cornwall?'

'I shall be going back soon.'

'I take it you've taken time off work. How is that, by the way?'

'Work is nonexistent. Literally. There

was a fire. The building's completely gutted; and as for the business, well I'm not sure where we're going from here. Poor Emily is thoroughly traumatised.'

The sudden silence on the other end of the phone made Carolyn wonder if the signal had gone. 'Hello? Henry?'

'Goodness me. I am sorry. Look, I've got to go, a customer's just walked in. I'll call you tomorrow. And please, I must see you again. Just coming, Mrs — ' And the phone went dead. He must have called from the shop.

Carolyn went outside to look for Jed, a confused expression on her face.

'So . . . are you going to see him again?' he said.

'He asked me to, but I've said no. I'm not sure I really want to go there again.'

'Up to you, of course. Maybe you would have heard why he wanted to leave you.'

'He says he'll phone me again tomorrow, but he was interrupted before I could tell him not to. He was really strange on the phone, too. I told him about the fire at work, and he just said, 'Goodness!' and then got off the phone. I would have thought it deserved a little more of a reaction that that!'

'It's probably not my place to say it, but he does seem a little self-involved.'

Carolyn nodded, still looking put out.

'Did you want some tea?'

'Oh, yes please.'

'I'll make it. The kettle's boiled, but I left you to your call. Won't be a minute.'

She saw a couple of letters lying beside Jed's seat. He'd obviously been reading them when she came out. He handed her a mug of tea and sat down again without speaking. After a few minutes, he spoke again.

'I've had a letter from the solicitor of the chap who own this place. Evidently he's decided to sell it. He's given me first option on it.'

'And will you buy it?'

'I very much doubt I could afford it. Remember, I told you it was falling apart when I moved in? He's now put it on the market at a ridiculous price. Oh, it may be worth it in a way, but I really feel cross he isn't allowing me anything for all the work I did.'

'That's terrible.'

'He paid for the larger things like the bathroom suite, and he also paid for the kitchen units, but I fitted them all. I did all the painting and decorating. And I renewed the plaster where it was needed. I did no end of stuff to improve the place. It would have cost him a fortune to get someone else to do it.'

'So what will you do?' Carolyn had forgotten her own worries with what Jed was saying to her. 'Will you make him an offer?'

'I don't think he'll even listen to me. Admittedly, I've had cheap rental from him for a year or two, but that was because I was working on the place. It seems he now wants to make his money and get me out.'

'But where would you live? If this place is sold, that means you'll have to start over again. Can't you afford to even consider it?'

'Not at his inflated prices. I suppose it'll be a case of having to start over.'

'Like me, you mean. I've got to face that, too. At least I own my flat outright. My parents left me enough money to buy it and have some left over. Paul's the same, of course. He owns his place.'

'Then you're both quite lucky. I've never had a great deal of money, and when I came down here I used it up before my business took off. Not much of a catch, am I?'

She smiled at him, thinking he was actually quite a catch for someone. He was so good-looking and seemed to have such a lovely personality, she could almost fall for him herself. She looked away, thinking she was quite stupid. She was still trying to get over Henry, wasn't she? Not helped by having seen him only that morning and hearing him on the phone so recently. But no, she was not going there again.

She had been well and truly hurt by him and would never risk it again. Jed seemed so different. So very nice and thoughtful in ways that Henry had never been.

'You didn't reply to my comment,' Jed said. 'You were supposed to argue like mad and say I'm a great catch.'

'I was thinking about it. Course you are. You're lovely and very good-looking. There, that has to be enough for now.'

'Thank you. All the same, I'm virtually broke and can't even afford to stay in my cottage. I really don't know where I should go next.'

'I'm sorry. Surely you could get a mortgage? All this stuff there is in the news about help to buy . . . '

'I've never given it much thought. Besides, I don't have a regular income. Well, not something I could write down and say, this is my annual income. Nor do I have much of a deposit.'

'I think you should try for it,' Carolyn advised him. 'Speak to the farmer or whoever it is who owns the place, and tell him what you've told me. He may listen. Without even trying, you're just rolling over on your back and waving your legs in the air.'

He laughed. 'Nice picture you paint. I'll think about it. But what about you? What are you going to do?'

'I don't think I want to see Henry again. Though I would like to know his reason for leaving the way he did. He was so mysterious about it.'

'Then go to meet him. You can take my car.'

'You wouldn't consider coming with me, I suppose?'

He looked uncomfortable. 'I don't think it's my place. It's something you have to do on your own, I'm afraid.'

'Like you, I'll think about it. Is there any more tea in that pot?'

He poured a cup for her and they sat in companionable silence, each one busy with their own thoughts. Jed was mentally going through his finances. He wondered how much he'd have to pay as a deposit and how much he'd have to borrow. The figures were daunting. He felt he was a good bet for repayments, but would anyone believe him?

Carolyn was thinking about Henry. She already knew he wanted to see her again, and she also knew he would try to persuade her to go back to him. She didn't feel she even wanted to go and see him. He was good-looking in his way, but even his looks seemed to have faded somewhat. He'd lost some of his confidence. In fact, he seemed to have lost most of it. What had happened to him? Why on earth was he working in a shop, with all his qualifications and previous experience? Perhaps she should see him again and find out what was going on with him.

'I think perhaps I should go and meet Henry,' she announced at last.

'Good. I think you should.'

'I can't persuade you to come too?' she almost begged Jed.

'No. You need to do this on your own.'

'But suppose he tried to persuade me to go back to him?'

'You have to follow your heart. I may not like it, but you must do whatever you think is the right thing. Borrow my car. I really don't mind.'

'Thank you. If you're sure. I don't know where he'll want to meet, but at least if I can get there, I won't let him know where you live. He's going to phone me later.'

'Fine. I'll go and get something ready for our supper.'

'I'll come and help. And Jed, thank you very much.'

'Whatever for?'

'For being so understanding.'

He didn't reply, but looked away. He was offering Carolyn his car to go and meet her ex-fiancé and possibly get back together with him. How would he feel if that happened? Gutted! But she needed to be sure of what she was doing, whether that be trying again with Henry, or making a fresh start with Jed. He would just have to trust that things would work out for the best in the end.

He couldn't say anything to express how he was feeling. 'What do you fancy for supper?' he muttered.

'Don't mind.'

'One of my concoctions it is, then.' He looked into the fridge and dragged out a pack of mince. 'Do you fancy chopping some onions? I'll make a spaghetti something-or-other.'

'Okay. Are you all right, Jed? Only, you seem a bit quiet. Quieter than usual.' He was concentrating on making his sauce and she felt concerned.

'I'm fine, thanks.' He went quiet again and she looked at him anxiously.

'I haven't said I *will* meet up with Henry again. Not to him, anyway.'

'You should see him if you want to. Don't mind me.'

'Actually, I do mind about you.' There, she'd said it. Not quite sure why, but she had. He stopped what he was doing and stared at her.

'I'm glad about that, very glad, but

you do have unfinished business with Henry. I'd feel better if I knew you wouldn't be tempted to go back to him, but I also feel you need to speak to him, to find out why he did what he did.'

'Oh Jed, I really don't think I could go back to him. But you're right, I do need some answers. I need to understand why he rushed away and why he's now working down here. You must admit, it really is something of a coincidence.'

'An 'of all the bars in all the world' sort of coincidence, you mean?'

'Well, yes. I find it amazing that we both should have come down here.'

'Maybe he had childhood holidays here.'

'Maybe. I'm not sure. Are these onions chopped finely enough for you?'

'They'll do. Can you open some tomatoes? There are some cans in the cupboard.' She did as she was asked, still thinking hard about what she should do.

She watched this man stirring the

pan of sauce. How did she really feel about him? How did he really feel about her? She knew she was attracted to him, and she really felt at ease in his company. Could she live with him indefinitely? Maybe. But then, she had felt that about Henry too; had been looking forward to sharing her life with him. Now she felt differently. She could see things had never been quite right, but she had been willing to compromise and hope it would all work out. But Jed was quite a different prospect.

10

Jed and Carolyn ate a quiet supper, both of them feeling somewhat subdued. She had heard nothing more from Henry and hadn't really expected him to phone her again. She wondered what he'd done with his mobile, but it had slipped out of her mind. He'd called her from the shop's phone so she hadn't really thought any more about it.

'I might turn in,' Jed announced eventually. 'I feel pretty bushed.'

'I wouldn't mind an early night myself,' Carolyn agreed. 'You go and I'll clear up the supper things.'

'If you're sure. Thanks. I'll go up and be out of your way in the bathroom.'

'Night, Jed. Sleep well.'

'You too.' He went up the narrow stairs and she heard him running the water and then his bedroom door shutting.

She washed up their few supper things and dried them, then opened the back door and stood looking at the moon. It was almost full and shone out brightly over the garden. She stepped outside, thinking how beautiful a place this was. The roses were all open and produced a heavenly scent. She heard a strange sort of grunting and felt alarmed for a moment, until she saw a hedgehog trotting along the path. She smiled at the little creature and spoke to him briefly.

When he disappeared under the bushes, Carolyn slumped down on one of the seats and thought about life, her own in particular. What was she going to do now that the company had burned down? She really must phone Emily and see how she was. She sat for a while longer and finally rose and went inside, her mind still running round in circles. How she was going to manage to sleep, she had no idea.

An hour later she was lying in her bed, still wide awake. She decided to go down and get a drink of water and see if she could find something to read. Jed must have something she might like. She went downstairs and poured herself a glass of water. Then she went into the lounge and looked along his bookshelf. She saw several things she had already read and was surprised to find they shared a number of authors they both liked. She picked up an old favourite and carried it back to her room.

'Can't you sleep, either?' Jed asked as she was going into her room.

She jumped and replied, 'Not really. I wasn't as tired as I thought I was. I sat out in the garden for a while. Did you know you had a hedgehog living out there?'

He laughed. 'Probably several of them. I often wonder how they ever get together. With prickles like those . . . '

'Very carefully, I'd say. I've borrowed one of your books. I hope you don't mind.'

'Course not. I was going to make some tea. Do you want some?'

'I suppose it might be better than water. I'll come down with you.'

It was almost midnight, and they went to sit in the comfortable seats in the lounge. Jed sipped his tea and at last he spoke. 'Carolyn, I've been thinking about Henry and you. Don't say anything till I've spoken, please. I said I didn't mind you seeing him again. But that's not strictly true.'

'But —'

'No, wait. Let me have my say. I've thought long and hard, and I've realised I don't want you to see him again. Of course I can't stop you if you really want to see him, but I'm scared. Scared of losing you. I know we don't have any sort of commitment to each other, but I'd like there to be. Well, some sort of commitment anyway. You see, I've fallen in love with you. I know we haven't known each other for very long, but I also know it's genuine love that I feel. There, I've said it now.'

She stared at him, her mouth falling slightly open.

'Well, go on, say something.'

'I don't know what to say.'

'Tell me I'm crazy, if you must. Better still, tell me you care just a little for me.'

'Oh Jed, of course I care for you. I'm still just wondering if it isn't a bit too soon. After Henry, I mean.' Jed looked positively crestfallen. 'I'm sorry,' she added. 'I do really care, and when a decent amount of time has gone by, I'm probably going to say I love you too.'

'If that's the best you can do, I'll be content with that. I'm just afraid that if you go back or if you see Henry again, he'll persuade you to return to him. I couldn't bear that.'

'Whatever he says to me, I won't go back to him. But you must realise everything I own, my whole life, is back in Buckinghamshire. My friends and family are all there. My work is there. Or rather it was. I don't know what's going on with Emily. And that's another thing — I've been so wrapped up in my time here that I've not called her yet to find out how she's doing and what's going on. I've decided to call her tomorrow and see what she's planning to do. You do understand all that, don't you?'

'I do. I'm disappointed, but I understand. Look, forget what I said. I'm going back to bed now.' He rose and went back to his room, leaving her sitting on the sofa, feeling even more confused.

'Oh Jed,' she whispered. She too rose and went back to her room. This time, she fell asleep quickly.

* * *

They were both asleep till after nine the next morning. Carolyn staggered downstairs feeling rather groggy. She reached for the kettle and filled it. She really needed coffee. Jed came down as the kettle boiled.

'Coffee?' she asked.

'Please. I didn't sleep much, did you?'

'I did, actually. Can't say my mind is any clearer today.'

'I meant what I said. I'm not hurrying you, but I needed you to know how I was feeling. Have you had any more thoughts?'

'I . . . well, I'm not sure I can talk about our future just yet. So much is up in the air. It's not that long since I was dumped at the altar, don't forget. And I really must phone Emily today.'

'To see if you still have a job, you mean?'

'Well, yes. And to find out how she is.'

'And if there is no longer a job, what will you do then?'

'I have no idea. Maybe I can get something else with another company. Or perhaps I should change my career totally. Be a shop girl,' she added wryly.

'You could always come and work for me.'

'Oh yes? Doing what, exactly?'

'I mentioned I was thinking of opening a shop or something. You could help me with pictures too. Oh, I don't know. Loads of things.'

'I'll add it to my list of things to think about. Have you thought any more about buying this place?'

'I'd like to, but I doubt whether anyone would lend me the money. I'm sure I could pay it back, but my earnings are pretty erratic. I can earn a small fortune one month and then go for two or three with low wages. Overall, I reckon I'm pretty safe.'

'Then you should go for it. Make an appointment to see someone.'

'You reckon?'

'Oh yes, certainly. Go for it.'

'Okay, I will.'

They had both finished their coffee, and Jed made some toast. They ate in silence, each busy with their own thoughts. When she had finished, Carolyn said she was going to speak to Emily. She dialled her number and waited. At last a sleepy-sounding voice answered.

'Hello?'

'Emily? It's Carolyn.'

'Carolyn? Oh yes, Carolyn.'

'How are you? Have you made any plans yet?

'Fine, dear. No, no plans.'

'So, what are you going to do about the company? Do I still have a job?'

'A job? What sort of job?'

'Emily, are you all right? You sound very strange.'

'I'm feeling rather unwell. Sorry, dear. I have to go now.' She disconnected the phone, and Carolyn turned to Jed with a worried expression on her face.

'Goodness, Emily sounded terrible. She could barely speak to me. I really think I should go back.'

'Okay,' said Jed, looking concerned. 'Is there someone else you can speak to, someone nearby who could go to see her in the meantime?'

'I suppose so. I'll call Sophie.' She looked at her phone and punched in the new number. 'Sophie? It's Carolyn. I wondered if you've been in touch with Emily?'

'I've tried, but she won't speak to me. Why?'

'I just called her and she seemed very strange. I wondered if you could go and see her, and call me back?'

'I suppose I could. I'm going for an interview this morning, but I could go round after.'

'An interview? Where?'

'Just another company in town. I didn't think anything was going to happen with Emily. She hasn't done anything about the company, has she?'

'I suppose not. Look, you've got my mobile number. If you do call round to see her, can you call and let me know how she is?'

'Okay. I must say, I'm disappointed to lose the job with her company. Can't afford not to work, though, hence my interview.'

'Okay. Bye for now.' Carolyn frowned and looked at Jed. 'Maybe I'll wait to see if she finds out anything and then consider what I'm going to do.'

'I'll take you back, of course.'

'That's good of you. But I can easily get a train. I don't want to drag you all that way.'

'Nonsense. Of course I'll take you. Let's wait to see what Sophie says.'

It was a slightly edgy day for both of them. Neither of them felt they could do anything much. At about three o'clock, the printer's rang Jed and said the brochures were ready.

'Think I'll go and fetch them. Then if we do go back to your place tomorrow, it won't be a hold-up.'

'Can I come with you?' asked Carolyn.

'Okay. Truro, here we come. I wondered about taking them round to Mrs Jacobs afterwards.'

'Fine by me. It'll mean we're both free tomorrow.'

They drove to Truro and collected the brochures. They did look wonderful, and Jed paid for them happily. He felt cheerful as they drove towards Penzance and the holiday complex.

'I'll keep a few back as advertising

material,' he said. 'Always good to have some of my own products to show people.'

Carolyn's phone rang and she answered it quickly without checking who it was.

'Hi, it's me. Just got a quiet moment in the shop.'

'Henry,' she mouthed to Jed. 'Hello, Henry.'

'I'd like to see you this evening. Please say you'll meet me. Or I can come and pick you up from wherever you are.'

'Oh dear. I'm not sure . . . '

'Please, Carolyn. Please come see me.'

'I might be going back tomorrow. I'm not sure yet.'

'Just one drink?' he urged. 'I really need to explain myself to you.'

'One drink, then.' She sighed. 'Where do you want to meet?'

'Do you know the Fisherman's Cove? It's a pub down by the coast.'

'Fisherman's Cove,' she repeated for

Jed's benefit. He nodded. 'All right. About nine o'clock. I'll see you then.'

'That's great. Thank you so much. I know it's going to be all right. We'll soon be sorted and back to normal.' He put down the phone before she could say anything else.

'Oh dear, he's definitely in organising mode,' Carolyn said. 'He seems to think it'll only take one drink for me to run back to him. Please, Jed, won't you come along?'

'I could come and sit in one of the other rooms, if you really want me to.'

'Oh yes, please. I'd really appreciate that. Just knowing you're nearby will make all the difference.'

'Hey, come on. It's only a drink with your ex-fiancé.'

'But I'm still thinking of what you said last night.'

'Last night was last night. I was probably over-emotional. In the cold light of day, it all seems so much clearer. I love you. You don't seem to love me. I'll get over it.'

'I never said I didn't. I'm still upset about being dumped, and a bit scared of getting dumped again.'

Jed stopped the car in the next lay-by. 'Carolyn, please don't think like that. It was awful that he left you the way he did, and clearly he had his reasons. But it was nothing to do with you as a person.'

'Maybe. All the same, it does hurt.'

'I know, love. But don't think all men are the same. Some of us are quite reasonable guys. Especially ones that are in love.'

'You keep saying that.'

'I want you to get used to the idea. Now, if we don't get on the road again, we'll never make it to the Fisherman's this evening.'

★   ★   ★

Mrs Jacobs was absolutely thrilled with her brochures when she saw them. 'They look marvellous,' she told them. 'You'll send me your bill, won't you?'

'Of course,' Jed said with a smile. 'I'm glad you like them. I'll finish your website along the same lines, shall I?'

'Yes please. I really am delighted with your work, Jed. Let's have a drink to celebrate.' She went to the fridge and produced a bottle of dry white wine.

'Only a very small one for me,' he said. 'I'm driving.'

'That's a pity. You could stay for supper with us . . . ?'

'I'm sorry, we have an appointment later. But thanks very much for the offer.'

'So, are you two . . . you know, together?'

'Not quite yet,' Jed told her. 'I have high hopes to persuade her, though.'

'Oh, I see. Playing hard to get, are you?' she teased.

'Not at all,' Carolyn replied, flustered. 'I . . . just . . . well, I'm not quite ready to commit.'

'I won't ask any more, my dear. You clearly have your reasons. But don't leave it too long or someone else will snap him up.'

'I think we might need to get on our way,' Jed said to Mrs Jacobs. 'Thanks very much for the wine, and sorry we can't stay for supper.'

'Perhaps we can arrange for you both to come another evening?'

'That would be lovely, thank you,' said Carolyn.

They drove back to Jed's cottage. The sky had clouded over and a few drops of rain began to fall. 'Looks like being a rather damp end to the day,' Carolyn observed. 'Is that usual in Cornwall?'

'It does seem to rain quite a bit. But it's what makes everywhere so green.'

It was raining heavily by the time they stopped. They both ran inside and got soaked on their way. 'Damn it,' said Carolyn. 'Why now? I'll have to change before we go out.'

'What do you want to eat?' asked Jed.

'I think I'm too nervous to eat much. How about something simple like cheese on toast?'

'Cheese on toast?'

'I love cheese on toast. What's wrong with that?'

'Not exactly much of a main meal.'

'Oh, do whatever you like. I'm going to change out of my wet things.' She ran upstairs and peeled off her soggy jeans. What should she wear? She really didn't want to look too dressed up, but she didn't want to look scruffy either. She was halfway into a different pair of jeans when her mobile rang. It was Sophie.

'Hi there, Carolyn,' she said. 'I went round to Emily's place. She's in a bad way. I think she's been drinking. Didn't want me to go inside her house at first, but I persuaded her. It really was a mess.'

'Oh dear, poor woman. Could you get anything out of her about the business?'

'Nothing. She isn't even thinking straight about her life, let alone work.'

'Have the police been in touch with her yet? Do they know any more?'

'She didn't say. I went round past the old building. It's pretty much been demolished. Safety, I suspect.'

'Well, thanks. I'll definitely be back in the next day or two. Oh, how did you get on with the interview, by the way?'

'I got the job. Start next week.'

'Well done! Congratulations, Sophie.'

'Thanks. I'll see you sometime. Mustn't lose touch.'

Carolyn finished dressing once she had disconnected. She did feel concerned for her old friend and colleague. In all honesty, Emily had been losing the plot lately. Carolyn had wondered if there was something wrong with her.

She went down to the kitchen, where she smelled wonderful aromas. 'What are you making?' she asked Jed.

'Wait and see. Did you get your call from Sophie?'

'Yes. It seems Emily's in a rather bad way. I'd like to go back quite soon.'

'Then so you shall, madam. Tomorrow or the next day?'

'Next day, I think. I may need time to

get over this evening, and won't want to dash off right away.'

'Sit down and eat. I've made you one of my special omelettes.'

'You're very good to me.'

'I know. I must be mad.'

11

They set off for the pub at around eight thirty. It was situated in a small village by the sea and the car park was fairly full. 'Anywhere left for you to park?' Carolyn asked.

'I'll have to leave it on the road a bit further away. You go on in, and I'll see you later. Good luck.'

'Thanks. I won't stay too long.'

'No worries.'

She got out of his car and watched as he drove away to park. She could so easily fall in love with him.

She went inside and spotted Henry immediately. It was a small bar and he was sitting at one side, a bottle of wine in front of him. 'Come and sit down,' he said. 'I got a bottle of your favourite wine. It's so good to see you again.'

'Thank you. Although I did say just one drink — and I meant it.'

'It's only one bottle.' He poured a large glass and handed it to her, then poured a smaller one for himself. 'Here's to us.'

She didn't raise her glass to that particular toast. She was looking for Jed, but he didn't come in. She sipped the wine. 'So what do you want to say?'

'First of all, I'm so sorry for leaving you the way I did. I really mean that. When I explain my reasons, I hope you'll forgive me.'

'I can't think of any reason why I should.'

'It was for your sake.'

'My sake? How on earth can you say that?'

'I sort of got involved in something a bit dodgy. I say sort of — I didn't actually do anything wrong, I want you to know that up front. There was this guy who started chatting to me in the pub. He knew all about me — where I worked, where I lived. He wanted me to alter some stuff on the computer system at work. I thought about doing it, I admit it — but when it came to it, I couldn't. So they threatened me.'

'Who did?'

'These guys he has working for him. Nasty people.'

'Whyever did you get involved with them in the first place?' Carolyn felt rather shocked.

Henry looked away. 'They promised me a lot of money. Said it would be enough to buy a nice house. I really wanted to please you, and agreed to their plan. But like I said, when I saw exactly what they wanted, I backed off and said I couldn't do it. These two blokes that work for him turned up on the morning of the wedding, and . . . well, I ran for it.'

'But you must have known they might do something like that when you first met up with them.'

'I wasn't thinking straight. It seemed like easy money.'

Carolyn sighed and shook her head. 'You really are an idiot. As if I ever cared about having a posh house. I love my flat. I'd never have been impressed by any of that.'

'I hated living in a home that was all yours. I wanted something that was ours. You must understand that.'

'I suppose so.'

'So . . . can we get back together? Please?'

'No! Henry, I'm sorry. I'm still fond of you, but you behaved stupidly, and you left me at the altar! I really don't feel the same about you as I once did.'

'It's that man you're living with, isn't it? It's only a week or two since we were about to be married.' His eyes had narrowed and he looked very angry.

'It's nearly two months ago.'

'Whatever. So, is it about him?'

'It's more about you. I really don't love you anymore. I'm sorry, but now I only feel relief we didn't go through with it. It's taken me a while to get to feel like that, but I do. And what you've just told me only makes it clearer.'

'But we could get it back, same as it was. I know we could.'

'You might, but I won't. As I say, I'm sorry.'

'Please, just think about it. We could sell your flat and find somewhere completely different together. Somewhere safe.'

'I'm sorry, Henry. I've given you my answer. I wish you well and hope you can be happy again at some point. And I won't be seeing you around here anymore. I'm actually going back home soon.'

'No!'

'What do you mean, no?'

'I just don't think it's safe for you.'

'Why?' asked Carolyn in shock.

Henry ran his fingers through his hair nervously. 'You told me your car was stolen and torched.'

'Yes, and . . . ?'

'And then your offices were burned down . . .'

Carolyn looked at him, aghast. 'Surely you don't think . . . ?'

Henry looked wretched. 'It's the only explanation. I think they're trying to warn me by targeting you. Please, Carolyn — sell your flat, and let's leave and make a new life together somewhere new.'

'I can't believe this! You put both of us in danger, and now you want me to sell my flat to bail you out?'

'Look, maybe you need some more time. I understand it's a lot to take in. All I know is, I'm going to have to leave. I can't stay here, in case they've followed you. I'll give you a call after you've had time to think about it all. It'll probably be a different number to the one you know. I can't use my mobile, in case it can be traced. I need to get a new one.'

Carolyn shook her head. At this point, she just wanted to be as far away from Henry as possible. To think, if things had happened another way, this was the man she would now be married to!

'I really must be going now,' she said, getting her bag and coat.

'But . . . there's still a lot of wine left.

Do have another.'

'I've had enough, thank you. Perhaps you could take it home with you. I'm sure the barman wouldn't mind. Goodbye, Henry. Good luck.'

He gave her a bitter smile. 'I'm going to need it,' he muttered, turning away from her and downing his glass, then pouring himself more wine.

Carolyn sighed and left him to it. She hoped Jed was nearby. She looked around outside and spotted him sitting on a wall, staring out to sea. He looked lost in thought.

'Penny for them,' she said, coming up behind him.

'Just wondering how you were getting on. What did he say?'

'I'll tell you on the way home. Let's get away now, before he comes out and follows us.'

'It was that bad, was it?'

'Worse.'

Jed caught her hand as they walked back to his car. She felt grateful to him for not pestering her about what Henry had said. She felt suddenly tired and somewhat emotional. It wouldn't take much for her to cry, and she swallowed hard, not wanting to break down. She sat quietly in the car as they drove back to Jed's cottage. He showed tremendous patience with her and said nothing.

'Do you want some coffee or tea?' he asked when they got in.

'You haven't got any chocolate, have you? I need a chocolate fix.'

'A drink, do you mean?'

'That'll do it.'

He soon came back with two large mugs of hot chocolate. 'There you are. Enjoy.'

'I should tell you about Henry's reason for running away.'

'Only when you're ready. You don't have to.'

Carolyn told him what Henry had said. He made no comment and listened carefully.

'And how do you feel about that?' he asked when she'd finished.

'I can't get over how stupid he was for getting involved in the first place. And I'm so angry that he could have put us in danger. Poor Emily — how can I ever tell her? To know that it might not have been an accident after all; that someone might have done this to her business on purpose . . . It could be the last straw for her.'

'So what will you do now?'

'I just think it's better to leave it all in the past. Oh, I can still remember some good times, but it was all a bit superficial. I'm much happier here with you.'

Jed blushed slightly. 'Does this mean you think we might have some sort of future together?'

Carolyn sighed. 'As Henry pointed out, it wasn't that long since he and I were planning on getting married.'

'Sorry.'

He looked so dejected that Carolyn took pity. 'Oh Jed! Yes, I think so. A definite maybe,' she joked.

'Okay. Enough said.' All the same, he

looked like the proverbial cat sitting in front of a pot of cream.

'I've finished my chocolate now. Thank you for that. I think it's way past my bedtime.'

'Okay. Off you go. I'll be up later. Are we going back tomorrow?'

'Can I decide in the morning? I feel absolutely worn out now. Can't make a sensible decision at this time of night.'

She went upstairs and got ready for bed, thinking about the evening. She'd never forget the conversation she'd had with Henry, or the shock and anger it had evoked in her. He really was now in the past. When she had come out of the pub and seen Jed sitting by the sea, she had known. She had felt so much relief seeing him. But somehow, she still felt it was all too soon. 'Rebound' was the word that sprang into her mind. All the same, she didn't want to lose Jed by procrastinating for too long. She tried to remember what he had said about his own life — that he was allergic to marriage. Well, he seemed to have changed his views somewhat.

She finished brushing her teeth and went through to her room. Though she felt exhausted, she couldn't fall asleep. Her mind was racing through the events of the day: Emily, Truro, then Mrs Jacobs, and finally meeting Henry.

'Go away, all of you,' she muttered, and turned over once more. This time she did go to sleep, and was troubled by dreams that caused her to wake several times.

★ ★ ★

'Wake up, sleepyhead,' said Jed, coming in with a cup of tea without milk — just how she liked it. 'I nearly came in earlier, but decided you wouldn't appreciate being woken.'

'What time is it?'

'Half past nine.'

'Oh goodness.'

'Doesn't matter. I was wondering how you feel about going back home?'

'Not mad keen, but maybe we should.'

'We could have a day on the beach and go tomorrow. It's a lovely day after the rain. Pity to leave it all behind, but of course, we can go if you want to.'

'You've persuaded me. Beach it is today, and we'll go back tomorrow — make an early start?'

'Okay. If that suits, ma'am. You do look lovely when you wake up.'

'I don't believe you,' Carolyn laughed. 'I look a wreck this morning.'

'You look tousled and still pretty sleepy. Do you want to sleep on a bit?'

'It's tempting. But no, I'll finish the tea and then get up. We shouldn't waste too much of the day. There are good beaches waiting for us. Can we have pasties again?'

'Presumably not from Henry's shop — at least, not for a while!'

'Oh. I forgot about that.' She gave him a sheepish grin.

'We'll go to another beach and find some on the way. There's a wonderful place about six miles away where they bake them on site. They're usually fresh out of the oven. We'll buy them and then eat them later on the beach. How does that sound?'

'Wonderful. Go away now and let me get up.'

'Don't be too long. I've got breakfast all ready for you.'

'What a wonderful man you are.'

'Yes, well don't you forget it.' He shot off downstairs again and she stretched out, luxuriating in the thought of a lazy day ahead with nothing much to do except enjoy it. She could smell bacon cooking. She rarely ate bacon, but it smelled so good she hurried through her ablutions and almost ran down the stairs.

'That smells wonderful,' she said.

'Thought it might get you down here. Go on out into the garden; I'll bring it out when it's done.'

'What luxury,' she told him. She went and sat at the little table and waited.

He soon came out with a large tray of

coffee and toast and two plates of bacon and eggs. 'Tuck in,' he invited her.

When they both had finished eating, Carolyn sat back, feeling very content. 'That was a lovely breakfast. Thank you very much.'

'My pleasure. I enjoyed it too. Now, let's wash up and get going. Do you like surfing?'

'Surfing? I've never tried it.'

'Then we shall go to a surfing beach. We'll hire a couple of boards and you can have a lesson.'

'I'm not sure I'd be any good. But I'll give it a try. I suppose you need good balance.'

'Well, yes. But that's when you try to stand. You need to do some body-boarding first. That's pretty easy, and you get a sense of finding the waves.' He was obviously quite keen.

'I'm not really sure. I'll happily go and watch you if you want to go.'

'Take your swimming things anyway and decide later. We'll still go to the surfing beach. I bet you won't be able to resist.' She said nothing and just looked at him quizzically.

They called for pasties en route to the beach, and their aroma filled the car. 'If I wasn't still full of breakfast, I'd eat mine right now,' Carolyn muttered.

'Then you wouldn't have it to eat on the beach. And you did say that was where you wanted to eat it.'

It was a beautiful day, and the beach Jed had chosen was indeed lovely. Carolyn did go into the sea, taking a board with her. She enjoyed the experience, but felt it would be a long time before she would ever be able to stand up like the experts.

It was late afternoon before they set off back to Jed's cottage. When they got there, Jed discovered several messages on the phone from his landlord. He was complaining that someone wanted to visit the place with the prospect of buying it but he couldn't let them in.

'Damnation,' Jed exclaimed. 'Now what do I do? I really don't want hordes of people coming here to look round. One of them might want to buy the place.'

'Oh dear, I am sorry,' Carolyn sympathised. 'Maybe I should go back by train. Then you can stay here to show people round.'

'But I don't want to show anyone round. And no, I won't let you go back by train.'

'You might have to. Why don't you phone your landlord and tell him you're going to be away and that it isn't convenient?'

'He'll insist on them coming in anyway. Though you're right — I'd better phone him anyway. Perhaps I can persuade him to leave it for a while.'

'I'll go and start my packing, ready for us to go tomorrow.'

He nodded and she went upstairs to collect her things together. She heard him getting quite heated as he spoke on the phone. She knew he really needed to live in this area because of his business. He was developing it quite well, and so anything she could suggest about him staying with her in Buckinghamshire simply wouldn't work.

'Not good news, I take it?' she said when she went downstairs again.

'Not really. He wants to have an open day this weekend and let everyone interested come in to look round. I'm sure someone will want to buy it. It's such a lovely place, it's bound to be popular.'

'Why don't you try to get a mortgage? I could actually lend you quite a bit; and with a decent deposit, you might manage to borrow enough to buy it.'

'I can't take your money. Bless you for offering, but I couldn't.'

'I told you, my parents left us quite a bit. I bought my flat outright and there's still some left. I'd only be lending it to you, not giving it. Go and see the bank tomorrow before we leave. See exactly what the situation is.'

'I suppose I could go and talk things through with them. At least I'd have some idea of what I might borrow. But it would mean we'd be rather later leaving.'

'Not to worry. It would be better to go with some idea of your future, don't you think?'

'Okay. I'll phone after breakfast tomorrow and see if they can see me. If you're sure you don't mind.'

'Course not. Shall I come with you?' Carolyn offered.

'Why not? Might be good for you to hear what he says.'

'What do you fancy eating? We've got various things in the fridge that need finishing. I could make something, if you like.'

'Now, am I willing to risk my life that way?' he laughed. 'I'll have to think about it seriously.'

'Cheek,' she giggled, punching him gently. He reached over and grabbed her hand. She hesitated and then relaxed. Gently, he tugged her closer and kissed her. She didn't resist, and kissed him back. Her senses were soaring in a totally new way ... like nothing she had ever felt before.

He let her go. 'Wow,' he said. 'That was something else.

'You're right,' she agreed. 'It was magical. I've never felt like that before.'

'Nor me. There must have been violins playing somewhere to accompany the feelings you stirred up.'

They both sat together and repeated their kiss. It was the same magical feeling again and again.

'If we really are going to have supper, we should stop doing this, however lovely it is, and get something ready,' Jed said reluctantly.

'Spoilsport,' Carolyn managed to utter. 'But you're right, as always. And we don't really want anything to get out of hand, now, do we?' He said nothing but studied her hard. 'What? What are you looking at?'

'You. Just you. You really are very beautiful, and the bits of sand still in your hair are even better.'

She laughed again and punched him

gently. 'You really know how to flatter a girl, don't you?'

'Let's cook something together,' he suggested, heading toward the kitchen. 'That way we might both stay healthy and even enjoy supper. I think there's some wine in the fridge. You can pour some for us while we cook.'

'Now that's the sort of cooking I really like.'

12

They made an appointment to see the bank manager at ten o'clock the next day. Jed took a collection of papers with him, as well as fairly feeble hopes. 'I really don't see him going along with this,' he said.

'You won't get anything from him with that attitude,' Carolyn chided him. 'Be positive. That way he'll have to listen.'

'But I really don't have much to offer as a deposit.'

'I can help with that, don't forget.'

'I've told you, I can't even think of accepting. Besides, repaying you would be a step too far. No, I think it's an impossible task. But I'll give it a go anyway.'

They parked a little way from the bank and walked through an alleyway. It was another glorious morning.

Carolyn felt almost reluctant to leave; but when she thought of the job she'd left behind — or rather, which had left her, she knew it was necessary. Then she remembered the previous evening and Jed's kisses. She thrilled at the thought and slipped her fingers into his free hand. He looked at her, slightly surprised. His warm brown eyes gazed smilingly into her own.

'This is a new phase we're entering, isn't it?' he said.

'I was just thinking about last evening, when you kissed me, and . . . '

'Sorry, but we're here. This is my bank.' He let her hand go and shuffled his papers in his other hand. 'Here we go. Let's see what the man can offer me.'

The meet-and-greet lady standing inside asked if she could help. When Jed told her about his appointment, she said, 'Take a seat for a moment. I'll see if Mr Blenkinsop is ready for you.' She reappeared a moment later.

'He'll see you now,' she said, ushering them into an office.

* * *

Jed looked rueful when they came out. 'I said it wouldn't do me any good, didn't I?'

'Oh I don't know,' Carolyn said. 'You can borrow about sixty percent of the amount you need. I can lend you the rest, if you'll only take it.'

'What I really need is to get the landlord to drop his price considerably.'

'That would be good. Why not let him hold his open day and see what comes out of it? Perhaps viewers won't offer him anything like the amount he's asking.'

'Maybe. It only takes one, though. Come on, we've got a long drive ahead of us.'

'I suppose so. It's so nice here, but there's so much I've got to sort out. I must go and see Emily. Oh, and there's a new car to buy. I'd almost forgotten about that delight.'

Three hours later, they were well on their way back to Buckinghamshire. Jed suggested they stop for some lunch, and Carolyn shrugged. 'If you like.'

'The inner man requires food,' he announced. 'There's a service station coming up in a few miles. Glorious motorway food should fill the spot.'

'Can't wait.'

The journey went on, and they were queueing in long traffic delays. They finally arrived at Carolyn's flat at about seven o'clock. There was a large heap of mail waiting for her, and she flicked through the envelopes.

'Oh, there's something from the car insurance company.' She opened it and exclaimed, 'That's good! They've offered me quite a large sum to spend on another car. I might even look at a brand-new one.'

'That sounds ideal. Shall we go out for something to eat? Save having to cook anything.'

'I suppose we could. There's nothing

much in the freezer. Just somewhere quick. I feel worn out — and you must, too, after driving all that way.'

'I do feel weary,' Jed said with a sigh. 'My brain is still humming along the motorway. Where shall we go?'

'There's a pub in the village. Nothing special, but it does reasonable food. And I want to call Emily this evening. I think I need to tell her what Henry told me.'

'Do you want to call her before we eat?'

'If you don't mind.' Carolyn dialled the number and waited. It seemed to ring forever and nobody replied. 'She must have gone out. That's encouraging, don't you think?'

'Probably, yes.'

'I'll try her again later. Let's go now and see what we can find to eat.'

She tried Emily's number several times during the latter part of the evening and finally gave up. 'I'll make us a drink, and then I think it's bed time,' she said. 'I'll have to wait till tomorrow to speak to her. What do you want, chocolate or coffee?'

'I'll go for chocolate, please. It feels strange to be a guest in your flat.'

'Well, don't feel strange. Please, feel at home here.'

'Thanks, I will. It's very different to my place, though. All on one floor, for starters. And it's very modern. But I do like it. I'm just used to, you know, older stuff.'

'I love your place. This is fine for me, though. Henry said he hated it, but I suspect that was because it was all mine.'

They drank their chocolate and went off to their beds. Carolyn fell asleep very quickly and woke feeling refreshed. She made tea and sat drinking it, remembering the days she had spent in Cornwall. She'd sat out in the garden on several occasions, something she couldn't do here. Would she like to live in Cornwall? She actually thought she would. Could she live with Jed? Oh yes, she decided. Yes, she could. The thought struck her that if she were to sell this flat, she could put the money towards Jed's cottage — if she were going to live there with him. Surely he couldn't object to that?

She pushed the idea to the back of her mind for the time being and decided to call Emily again. She must be home by now, Carolyn reasoned. But again, there was no reply. Worried, she dialled Sophie's number.

'Hello, Sophie, it's Carolyn. Do you know what's happening with Emily?'

'Oh Carolyn, I'm so sorry — I haven't had chance to call you. It's pretty bad, I'm afraid. She tried taking an overdose. Luckily I went round to see her the same day and found her.'

'Oh no! Oh, poor Emily. And how horrible for you. Is she all right now?'

'Physically, yes, but she's in rather a state.'

'Is she still in hospital? Can she have visitors?'

'Yes, and yes.'

'I'll go and see her later today. I'm so sorry you had to go through all this. I should have been here for her.'

'Don't worry about it. I'm just glad I was able to do something.'

The two ex-colleagues chatted for a while longer, and when Carolyn heard Jed moving around, she said she had to go. She re-boiled the kettle and presented him with some tea when he appeared.

'Service with a smile, eh?' he said, leaning over to kiss her. 'Sleep well?'

'Jed, something's happened. It's Emily. She tried to kill herself. She's still in hospital. I'm going to call and find out when I can visit. I really need to go and see her — I feel awful that I wasn't here for her. Will you be all right?'

'Of course. But I'll drive you. You haven't got a car, remember.'

'No. I must go to the garage and get that sorted out.'

'Let's do it this morning. And do we need some shopping?'

'The oh-so-practical Mr Jed Soames. Yes, I do.'

'I'd also like to call Paul; see if they're free for the evening. And I suppose I should speak to the parents. I ought to go and see them.'

'Oh yes, of course. Where do they live?' Carolyn asked.

'Out towards Rugby. It's quite a longish way, so I'd need to go for a whole day.'

'You go off whenever you like. I can always hire a car to run around in.'

'Maybe tomorrow, then?' he suggested. 'I'll call them later and see if they're around. You could always come with me.'

'I think you ought to go on your own, actually. You can tell them about me if you want to.'

'Really? That sounds almost promising.'

'Maybe,' Carolyn said with a smile. 'You simply never know what'll happen, do you?'

Having called the hospital and found

out visiting times for the afternoon, they headed to the garage and looked at several new models. Carolyn found something similar to her old car, which the garage ordered for her, and in the meantime she left with a nice little hire car to drive away in, courtesy of her insurance. They left one very happy salesman behind them.

'Do you want to go back to the flat?' Carolyn asked. 'I can always do the shopping on my own.'

'What, and deprive me the total pleasure of the supermarket visit? Certainly not. I wouldn't miss it for the world. You lead the way in your new hire car and I'll follow.'

They set off together along the road, and Carolyn parked some distance from the crowded shop. Jed joined her, and they soon filled the trolley.

'I'm going to get some flowers to take to Emily,' Carolyn said. 'What do you think?'

'Perfect.'

They added a bunch and went to the

checkout, Carolyn insisting on paying this time, then drove back to the flat and took in the shopping.

'I'll go out with my camera this afternoon,' said Jed, 'and leave you to go to the hospital on your own. Now you're an independent driver again.'

'Fine by me. There are some nice walks around.'

'I've been here before, remember. I lived here for quite a while.'

'Sorry. I just think of you as living in Cornwall. Hard to remember you once were a city boy.'

It seemed strange to be on her own for the first time in a while. She drove to the hospital and asked at the desk which ward Emily was in. She felt totally shocked when she saw her friend and former boss. Emily looked positively emaciated, and somehow shrunken. Carolyn fixed a smile on her face and tried not to let her shock show.

'Emily, it's so good to see you. I've brought you some flowers. Sorry I wasn't able to come earlier, but I was in Cornwall.' Then she ran out of anything to say.

'I am sorry, my dear. I've been so silly. It seemed the only way out. I do feel foolish. Couldn't even do this one thing satisfactorily.'

'You must have felt desperate, I understand that. I was pretty low myself when Henry ran out on me.'

'You seem to have got over that all right. I must say, you look better than I've seen you in ages.'

'I am. But how about you? How do you feel now?'

'Foolish, as I said. The fire . . . it's all my fault. I must have left something on.'

'No, Emily,' Carolyn began, feeling awful about what she had to tell her.

Emily sighed, and a tear rolled down her cheek. 'Things haven't been going so well lately. It's not like I haven't thought how nice it would be to just sell up and be free of the worry of it all.'

'You mean . . . you left something on,

on purpose?' said Carolyn, confused.

Emily looked distressed. 'I think I must have done! I didn't mean to — but I can't think of any other way it could have happened. What if I did it, you know, subconsciously?'

'Oh Emily, no — that's really not it at all.' Carolyn explained the whole sorry mess to her erstwhile boss, who sat and listened. When she finished, there was a silence as Emily processed what Carolyn had told her.

'So . . . I didn't start the fire?'

'I very much doubt it, Emily. And I'm so sorry not to have been more supportive — I just never realised anything was wrong with the business. You always seemed to be on top of everything.'

'Nothing is quite as it seems.' Emily shook her head ruefully, then took a breath. 'Now, tell me about your stay in Cornwall. It sounds lovely.'

For the next few minutes Carolyn talked of the lovely places she'd seen, and of Jed's cottage.

'And this Jed — is he the new man in your life?'

'I think he may be. I did see Henry while I was there. He's working in a shop. Strange, but he said he's enjoying it.'

'That doesn't sound like your Henry.'

'He isn't my Henry. Not at all.'

'I'm so glad to hear it. I never felt he was right for you. Always seemed a bit . . . sly, I suppose.'

'Goodness. You never let on that you didn't like him.'

'I'll never forget the look on your face when you ran into the church that day. You looked like a real firecracker.' She smiled. 'I wouldn't have liked to be on the receiving end of it when you found him.'

'Well, luckily for him I'd calmed down a lot by the time I did!'

'You know something, my dear — I feel much better for having talked it all through with you. I've been feeling so guilty.'

'You do look better. I felt so worried

when I came in and saw you lying there. You've nothing to feel guilty about, you know.'

'I will have to speak to the police and see what they have to say about all this. And the insurance will hopefully pay me something for the business. I might just retire now. Start doing things I never had time for. I do feel so bad about my staff, though. Perhaps they'll give me enough to allow me to pay them something . . .'

'Don't worry about it,' Carolyn said gently. 'They'll all get jobs soon enough. Sophie's got one already.'

'Did you know I'm going home tomorrow?'

'I'll come and fetch you if you like,' Carolyn offered.

'Oh, don't worry, I can get a taxi. Or maybe they'll send me home in one of their vehicles.'

'Nonsense. What time are you due to be discharged?'

'After lunch. I have to see the psychiatrist before I go.'

'Right. So if I come about the same time as today . . . ?'

'Well, thank you very much. If you're sure.'

The arrangements were made. Carolyn would buy a few basics to see Emily home, so whatever Jed was doing, he'd have to do it on his own. This was important to her and she wanted to know she'd done her best for her old boss.

★ ★ ★

'It looks as though I'm in the job market again,' Carolyn told Jed over supper. 'Emily's thinking of taking early retirement, so all of us are free now.'

'My offer of working with me in some sort of shop is still open,' Jed reminded her. 'I think it might be rather nice to work together. You could soon learn to help me, too, seeing how well you worked when we were doing the brochures for Mrs Jacobs.'

'I didn't do much. But I don't know

. . . Working in a shop all day doesn't really appeal much. Besides, it'd mean I'd have to move to Cornwall.'

'Would that be so hard?'

Carolyn shrugged. 'I don't know. Maybe not. I do love it there. Actually, I was thinking . . . If I sell this place, maybe you'd accept the money towards buying your cottage? Though then I'd have nowhere to live. I suppose I could come and live with you, and we'd just have to get married!'

He stared at her, almost disbelieving what he was hearing. 'Do you mean that? Really?'

She burst out laughing. 'Of course I do. I love you, Jed. Don't look quite so amazed. You're a very loveable guy. Oh dear, I've just remembered — you told me when we first met that you're allergic to marriage.'

'That was after Gemma left me in the lurch. Besides, I thought you were pretty much against marriage yourself.'

'That was because of Henry. I was a bit sensitive at the time. In fact, the day

Paul introduced us, it was my first outing as a single woman.'

'Well, you managed it very well. See? I fell in love with you right away. We need to go out to celebrate. I'll call Paul and Mel. They can join us tomorrow night. We'll have us a banquet.'

'Don't forget, I'm going to collect Emily from hospital tomorrow afternoon. I wondered if you might want to go to see your parents while I'm out?'

'I shall postpone that trip till you have time to come too. Now that we're planning to live together, they'll need to see you.'

'Live together? I suppose we must be. So, can I assume that means you do want to marry me?'

'I will consider it carefully and let you know.'

She looked at him, somewhat shocked, but said nothing. Maybe he really was allergic to marriage. Was he joking? She couldn't tell. And, worse, the subject seemed to be dropped for the rest of the evening. So much for her making assumptions. Carolyn knew she really ought to say something to Jed, but she couldn't.

'Shall I call Paul and invite them out tomorrow, or will you?' she said at last.

'I'll call him if you like.'

Carolyn listened as he spoke to her brother. She was expecting he would tell Paul about their engagement, but he said nothing. She felt ridiculously hurt.

'So, we'll see you tomorrow evening, then,' Jed said as he finished the call. 'Oh, Carolyn sends her love, by the way. Bye.' He hung up.

'I'd have liked a word or two, actually,' she told him.

'Sorry, I wasn't thinking. Never mind, we'll see them tomorrow. You can have all the words you want then. Now, I'm going to wash up and then turn in. Is that all right with you?'

'I can do the clearing up. You go to bed, if you're tired.'

'No, I'll get this done first. You can dry and put away.'

She watched Jed as he efficiently finished the washing-up and left everywhere very tidy. He went up to bed and she followed a short while later, her thoughts running round in small circles. Had she misinterpreted what he felt about her?

13

Jed went off on his own again the next day, clutching the cameras he'd brought to photograph various local scenes. He said nothing about Carolyn's suggestion that they should plan a wedding, and she certainly didn't want to raise the subject again. She had to admit, she felt rather hurt by his reaction.

She went to collect Emily from the hospital after calling at the stores first to buy bread and milk and one or two treats for her friend and ex-boss. She went to the ward and saw Emily was ready to go. Her little suitcase was packed and stood by the bed.

'This is very good of you, Carolyn. I do appreciate it.'

'No problem. Looks as if you're ready to go.'

'Yes, I am. Glad to get out of this place, actually. The nurses are mostly very kind, but one of them told me I was bed-blocking or something similar. Perhaps I should have made a better attempt at it and saved them the bother.'

'Come on. If they hear you saying things like that, you'll be sent off somewhere else.'

'Oh don't worry, I won't try it again. And I'm never going to drink again. I drank nearly half a bottle of something or other. I scarcely knew what I was doing.'

'Oh, Emily.'

'You know, I can't tell you how glad I am I was unsuccessful. Life is certainly not all that bad.'

'I'm glad to hear it.'

Carolyn put Emily's bag in the back of her car and drove them back to Emily's home. It took only minutes to get there, and Carolyn wished she'd thought of going there previously, if only to air it out before the owner's return. They went inside and Emily gasped in surprise. There were several lots of flowers, and everywhere was sparkling clean. There were even supplies in the fridge, making Carolyn's purchases redundant.

'Oh my goodness. Who has done all this?' Emily said, quite overwhelmed.

'There's a card on the shelf. Open it and see what it says.'

Emily did so. 'Oh, how lovely. The girls from the office have done it all, and it says, 'Wishing you a speedy return to your usual excellent health. With Love from Sophie, Annabel and Mary.' Isn't that nice?'

'Yes, what a wonderful surprise. I've got you a few bits and pieces too. I'll put them in the fridge for you. Would you like a cup of tea?'

'That would be lovely, dear. Thank you very much. But I can do it, you know.'

'Of course you can, but make the most of me while I'm here. I somehow don't think I'm going to be around all that much longer. I'm thinking of moving to Cornwall.'

'Cornwall? Whyever are you going there? I thought it was just a holiday place.'

'People do live there too, you know,' Carolyn said, laughing.

'Is this something to do with the young man you met?'

'Jed. Yes.'

'Jed's a funny name. What's it short for?'

'I've no idea. I assumed he was called Jed. I'll have to ask him.'

They drank their tea, and at last Carolyn said it was time she was leaving. 'I'll call you later on; make sure you're settling in okay.'

'Thank you very much, Carolyn. But you've no need to worry.'

'I'm glad to hear it. But I'll still call later. Bye now, Emily.'

She drove home and looked for Jed's car. It wasn't parked outside. She shrugged and went back inside her flat. It was undisturbed and looked just as she had left it. Whatever he was doing, he hadn't returned since she left.

She went into her room to try to decide what to wear that evening. It might be quite an occasion, so she didn't want to look anything less than smart. Mel always looked good, she thought, and she didn't want to let anyone down. She tried on several outfits before deciding on a short black cocktail dress. She sighed, remembering it was the one she wore for her engagement party. It most certainly would not do for this evening. She really needed something different. Then she remembered some of the new things she had bought for the honey-moon. She foraged in the wardrobe and came out with a deep-blue silky dress. It was strapless, and hopefully would be ideal. She tried it on and pirouetted in front of the mirror. This was the one. She'd never worn it before, and it seemed perfect.

'Anyone at home?' Jed called.

'Just coming,' she called back, quickly stripping off the dress and pulling on her jeans again. 'How did you get on?' she asked as she came downstairs.

'Fine. How was Emily?'

'Okay. She told me she'd got herself drunk before she took the pills and didn't really know what she was doing. Promised me she'd never try it again.'

'And do you believe her?'

'Yes, she seemed to be in earnest. I think it was a mixture of shock, alcohol, and misplaced guilt. I really do think she'll be fine. So, have you decided where we're going this evening?'

'I thought the pub near here. Paul and Mel will come here first and give us a lift.'

'Oh, I see.' Her blue dress was much too dressy for the pub. She felt slightly disappointed. 'I'd better go and choose something to wear,' she said.

'Make it something smart,' Jed suggested.

'Not too smart for that pub. I'd get drummed out for indecent exposure.'

'Why? What were you thinking of wearing?'

'Oh, just a new sundress. I'll maybe go for jeans and a nice top instead.'

'The sundress sounds nice. Wear that.'

'Bit dressy for the pub.' She didn't notice the twinkle in his eye.

'Well I'm going to wear my new suit, and I've even bought a tie.'

'New suit? And a tie? Isn't that a bit much?'

'Only the best for my lady.'

'Where are we really going? It isn't the pub, is it?'

'No. You're all too easy to tease. We have a table booked at the Pink Pelican. Very exclusive, don't you know. Ties are always worn as a matter of course.' He spoke in such a silly posh voice, she soon collapsed into laughter.

'That sounds lovely. Wonderful, in fact. Thank you. Do Paul and Mel know we're going there?'

'They do indeed. They offered to collect us so we don't have to worry about driving. Is that agreeable to you, madam?'

'Yes, absolutely. But won't they want to drink?'

'Mel's flying off in the morning, so she needs to stay sober. I'll go and change now. That's where I was all this afternoon. Buying my new suit.'

'I see. And what time are we going out?'

'They're getting here for seven o'clock.'

'Then I'd better go and start getting ready too, hadn't I?'

'You had indeed. I could do with a shower. I got very warm in the shops, in and out of different clothes. Could have done with you there to help me, really, although that would have ruined the surprise a bit! I hope you like it.'

'I'm sure I shall. Go on then, go and shower.'

She heard him singing as he showered. He sounded happy, and she smiled with pleasure. While he was busy, she took the opportunity to call and check on Emily. And Emily had some news of her own.

'Oh Carolyn, you're not going to believe it! I've heard from the fire investigation people, and it was faulty wiring that was to blame!'

'What?' said Carolyn, her brain whirling.

'It was the wiring! It wasn't my fault, and it wasn't some kind of grisly mobster-style warning — it was just an honest-to-goodness accident! I can't tell you how much lighter I feel.'

'So the whole thing — my car, the factory — it was just coincidence and bad luck!'

'Yes, my dear. Though seeing as it's scared Henry off, maybe not such bad luck after all. At least now you can keep buying your honey without having to worry about bumping into him!'

Carolyn laughed and said her good-byes to her old boss, promising to call in a few days to find out how everything was going. She changed into the blue dress and fixed a narrow gold chain round her neck. She couldn't decide what to do with her hair. It looked much lighter than before her holiday in Cornwall, and she quite liked it. She brushed it and left it loose. It looked nice, she decided. A quick touch of lip gloss and she felt that she was ready.

She went downstairs and saw Jed standing in the lounge, holding a glass of champagne. 'Goodness me,' she said.

'I wanted to start the evening well,' he told her.

'It looks as if you've scored highly already. I love the suit. And the tie is also perfect. Exactly what I'd have chosen.'

'I'm glad.'

'So, what should we make a toast to?' Carolyn asked him.

'Nothing, really. I just fancied treating us to something pleasant to drink.'

'Oh, I see.' She tried to hide her disappointment.

'You ready for a top-up?'

'I'll be totally drunk before we get too much further.'

'Then I'd better ask you now.

Carolyn, will you marry me?' he said as he went down on one knee.

Her eyes filled with tears and she held out her hand to him. 'I will.'

He got up and said, 'I hope you like this ring. If you don't, we can go and change it tomorrow.' From his pocket he took out a small box and opened it. He held out a ring she fell in love with on first sight.

'Oh, it's beautiful. I love it.' He slipped it onto her finger and it was a perfect fit. 'Oh thank you. Thank you so much.'

'Good. I took a bit of a risk, but glad you like it.'

'How did you know what size to get?'

'I'm afraid I was a bit naughty. I looked in your dressing-table drawer and found the old one. Henry's ring, I suppose it was. I borrowed it and took it with me to the jeweller's. Hope you don't mind.'

'I think that was pretty ingenious of you. Well done.'

'Here's the old one back, by the way.

You might want to put it back in your dressing table.'

'I must admit, I'd quite forgotten it was there. It's a shame I didn't get chance to give it back to Henry. He could probably have done with the money it would fetch! Oh Jed, I really love my ring. Thank you.'

He smiled. 'I think Paul and Mel should be here any time. They don't know anything about our plans yet, so it'll be a surprise to them.'

'I think Paul will be slightly shocked, actually.'

'Maybe. I doubt it, though.' The doorbell rang. 'I'll let them in, shall I?'

'Please. Gosh, what a day this is turning out to be.'

Jed let them in and, nearly bursting with his news, said, 'We've got something to tell you. We're engaged! Have some champagne to help us celebrate.'

'Well done, sis!' Paul exclaimed. 'I'm so pleased. Congratulations to both of you. Thanks,' he said as he grabbed a glass from Jed.

'Yes, congratulations,' echoed Mel. 'When's the big day?'

'Nothing planned yet,' Jed replied. 'It's only just happened.'

'But you've got a ring already?'

'Yes, isn't it gorgeous?' Carolyn held out her hand for Mel's inspection.

'Very elegant. It suits you.'

'Here's to you both,' said Paul. 'May you be very happy and enjoy your lives together. Actually, it's kind of a double celebration — we're planning to get married pretty soon too!'

'Well, congratulations!' Jed laughed, beaming from ear to ear. 'About time, too. How long have you been together now?'

'Years and years,' Mel told them. 'I'm getting a new job. Just short runs, to the continent and back in the same day. It'll make such a difference to us.'

'Looks like we'll all be making huge changes to our lives,' Carolyn said.

'Perhaps we should consider a joint wedding,' Jed suggested. 'Save on the cost of it all.'

'Well, actually, we're just planning a small do at the local registry office,' Paul told them. 'Just one or two friends and a meal afterwards. Next weekend!'

Jed's eyes widened. 'Next weekend! You don't waste time, do you, mate?'

'No point. It's about time I made an honest woman of her.'

'Hey you,' Mel retorted, 'just watch what you're saying.'

'And we'll have our wedding pretty soon too, won't we?' Carolyn said.

'I suppose so. Not next weekend, though!' Jed laughed. 'Wow, we really have something to celebrate, don't we?'

'Certainly do,' Carolyn said. 'Let's get this show on the road. You okay to drive us, Mel?'

They went off to the restaurant, where the staff were all primed about the engagement party. It was an excellent evening, and by the time they all got back to Carolyn's flat, they were very merry.

'Tell me something, Jed,' Carolyn said. 'What's 'Jed' short for?'

'You don't want to know.'

'Oh, but I do. Come on. Do you know, Paul?'

'I've no idea.'

Jed closed his eyes. 'You'll never believe it.'

'Come on, then.' Carolyn smiled. They were all listening avidly.

'It's Jermyn Daniel — JD or Jed for short. The only people in the world who call me Jermyn are my parents. Now do you see why I was hesitant about taking you to see them?'

'What's wrong with that as a name?' Carolyn asked him.

'It's so . . . unheard of. Anyway, forget I told you. I don't want ever to hear it from any of you again.'

'Okay, Jermyn. We'll forget it immediately, if not sooner,' Paul teased. 'Come on, love, we'd better go if you're to get your flight in the morning.' They said good night and went off.

'Jed, if I'm coming to Cornwall,' Carolyn began, 'please won't you accept the money from me for your house? I can't bear to live anywhere but in the cottage.'

'I really don't like to . . . '

'I'm going to put this place on the market, and if you don't accept my money, then I shall be the first person to bid for your cottage when it goes on the market.'

He laughed. 'In that case, thank you very much. I'll phone the landlord in the morning and make him an offer.'

'Good. And I think that concludes the business for today.' She giggled before she hiccupped loudly. 'Heavens, I think I must be drunk.'

'I love you, Carolyn Brown, drunk or not.'

'And I love you, Jed Soames.'

HER HEART'S DESIRE
FROM THIS DAY ON
WHERE THE HEART IS
OUT OF THE BLUE
TOMORROW'S DREAMS
DARE TO LOVE
WHERE LOVE BELONGS
TO LOVE AGAIN
DESTINY CALLING
THE SURGEON'S MISTAKE
GETTING A LIFE
ONWARD AND UPWARD
THE DAIRY
TIME FOR CHANGE

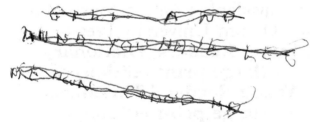

We do hope that you have enjoyed reading this large print book.

Did you know that all of our titles are available for purchase?

We publish a wide range of high quality large print books including:
Romances, Mysteries, Classics
General Fiction
Non Fiction and Westerns

Special interest titles available in large print are:
The Little Oxford Dictionary
Music Book, Song Book
Hymn Book, Service Book

Also available from us courtesy of Oxford University Press:
Young Readers' Dictionary
(large print edition)
Young Readers' Thesaurus
(large print edition)

For further information or a free brochure, please contact us at:
Ulverscroft Large Print Books Ltd.,
The Green, Bradgate Road, Anstey,
Leicester, LE7 7FU, England.
Tel: (00 44) **0116 236 4325**
Fax: (00 44) **0116 234 0205**